LOCKED

K.L. STEELE

Edited by: ProofsbyPolly

Cover design by: © Dez Purington @ Pretty in Ink Creations

Artwork by: Priska (@Priska_art)

Proof Edit by: SpooksProofs

This one is for everyone who pushed me to follow my dream rather than hide from it, and to those who supported me every step of the way. I made it here because of you.

Content Warning

If you know me personally, now is your chance to put the book down. Please and thank you.

Locked is on the darker side of romance, with a number of scenes/situations that may be uncomfortable for some readers. It is a plot-light introduction to the Blackstone Gates world, with a hefty dose of blood and hand necklaces. The characters in this book are all over the age of 18 years. Please be aware that this novella contains:

Blood play

Knife play

Self-harm

Somnophilia

Dubcon/noncon

Explicit sex scenes

Biting

Marking

Shared releases

Multiple partners/group scene

Breath play/choking

Sexual acts in monster form

PROLOGUE
LUKA

The adrenaline of the chase courses through my veins as I watch Bale hunt the hellhound below me on foot. Both of us are born hunters, and if it wasn't for the fact that we were here on a mission from our father, we would likely enjoy ripping these assholes to shreds a little more. The low-lying mist that surrounds Blackstone Academy, paired with the dark pink hue of the dusk sky, makes it slightly more difficult to see the pair, even with my heightened senses.

I track them from just above the trees, watching closely as Bale swipes his hand out, missing the beast by a whisper. He weaves his way through the dense woods, the obsidian-black hound just out of his grasp. His kind are extremely agile, with reflexes well beyond most other supernatural beings.

This is the fourth hellhound hunt we've had in the last six months, and both of us are getting fucking tired of it. Students that enter the woods surrounding the academy are torn to pieces and left behind as unrecognizable corpses for us to clean up.

I had tried to beg our father to let me in on the meetings with the families. The raw emotion in the room would have been heaven to siphon, but Headmaster Pierce is the only one allowed to dole out the bad news. It's bullshit if you ask me, but what do I know?

Coursing through the mist, I pull my black wings tight against my back and drop down in front of the beast, halting him in his tracks. My body jolts on impact as I land, tensing immediately when faced with the sheer size of the hound. I suck in a deep breath, preparing for the carnage that is sure to happen. A single look at my twin and his manic smile behind the hound tells me all I need to know about how this is going to go.

While I'm confident that we can take him down easily, hell-hounds are unpredictable and irrational. My hands fly up, palms facing the beast, in an attempt to show we are not here to attack straight off the bat. As much as Bale would love that, we need information from him first.

Where I am fairly rational, well as much as a demon can be anyway, Bale thrives in the chaos. His bloodlust overtakes any rational thought half of the time.

He approaches the beast from the tree line, his menacing, amber eyes looking over him in detail and taking in anything that we can report back to identify the asshole.

Smoke pours from the hound's black coat as he looks around, assessing his escape plan. He's covered in scars, the thick slashes marring his face while his coat has lightened, white patches. Most of them look older, the hair having grown back a lighter shade in some areas, but there are a number of marks on his face that look extremely fresh. This thing is bigger than the last few have been, his coal-like eyes level with my own.

"Who's fucking sending you here?" I growl, stepping closer and watching him snap his teeth toward me in response. We've fought demons much more terrifying than him, so his efforts to strike fear fall flat. A gravelly howl tears through him as Bale rips his claws across the hound's heels, forcing him to collapse on the cold, damp ground before he can retaliate.

The two of us circle him while he tracks us with his glowing, ember-filled eyes, unable to rise because of his wounds. Someone is sending these beasts up through the gates for something, and we need to figure out who it is, fast.

"They have us coming through the gates of hell, and they send two kids to kill us off? Cute." He laughs, his breathing steadying as his fresh wounds start to heal. Hellhounds have healing abilities, so Bale's slashes will heal, given that they were a fresh cut with no supernatural power used. The cuts on the arrogant mutt's face, on the other hand, look to have been done by a demon, one with enough power to stall the healing process.

"Who." Slice.

"Fucking." Slice.

"Sent." Slice.

"YOU?" Bale roars, tearing his long, sharp claws into the beast's back with every word. He growls in response, gnashing his teeth in Bale's direction but missing him completely, frustration marring his scarred face.

He starts to shift toward me, his lips pulled into a snarl as he drags himself off the ground slowly. Bale's cuts are obviously not deep enough to slow him down for long.

"You boys don't stand a chance in hell itself to win this. Run back to daddy where you belong and off this plane before we tear it to the ground to find her."

My eyes meet Bale's; a silent nod between us is all we need to finish off this asshole and send him to purgatory. As twins who have been hunting together since we could walk, we have this dance down to a fine art.

Bale locks his claws into the hellhound's shoulder blades and lengthens his fangs as he pulls its head to the side with his other hand. Blood covers his face as he sinks his teeth into its neck, tearing out a piece of smoking flesh and dropping it onto the forest floor.

"Fuck, these assholes taste like shit," he laughs before ripping its head to the other side and piercing his fangs into the hound's throat, holding him in place for me.

My form comes out to play, towering over the beast while it thrashes in Bale's grasp. Piercing my tail forward, I slice the razor-sharp edge across his throat, forcing a gurgling sound from his mouth. His eyes widen, embers from the burning coal escaping rapidly into the cool air. Bale rips his teeth away with force, taking a piece of flesh with him as smoke billows out of the large wound. He tears into its chest with his clawed hand and removes its warm, beating heart with a wide grin on his face.

A sudden feeling rushes over my body, unlike anything I've ever felt before. By the look on Bale's face, having dropped from a sinister grin to a scowl, he must feel it too. The wind carries a scent, sweetness and sin all wrapped into one. It has to be her. My chest is heaving, needing to take a few deep breaths before I do something stupid like run to her covered in hellhound blood.

"It fucking can't be. Father is full of shit. She doesn't exist," he growls out before turning to walk back to the academy.

"Brother, I can scent her. She's here."

CHAPTER ONE
WYNN

It turns out that burning down the entire school after years of being bullied relentlessly isn't the correct way to handle things. They were forced to close the doors for months, with the repairs alone costing them millions. My parents had filtered enough money into the place to keep me enrolled up until now, despite my behavior being frowned upon by the board for the last few years.

My personal favorite was the time when I released a plague of locusts into the cafeteria, screaming at the top of my lungs that they were flesh-eating bugs. Little did the entire school know that the innocent little things don't typically eat humans, but it was worth the chaos to watch the school scramble. A grin spreads across my face at the memory, their looks of horror etched into my mind permanently.

I was the outcast, the last one picked in groups. The one that students would sneer at and bullies targeted from day one. The teachers turned a blind eye for years, not wanting to get involved for fear of potentially getting on the bad side of the founding families. The same families that brought their children up to frown upon those who are different.

My parents started paying off the board early on, increasing their contributions each time something went wrong or I fought back. Now here I am, on my way to a new school, Blackstone Academy, to finish off my final year. The place where they send misfits, and kids that aren't wanted anywhere else.

This should be fun.

The sleek, black Escalade rolls to a stop outside of a set of tall, wrought-iron gates as two men exit the building off to the side. Tactical gear clings to their overly muscular frames, with holsters carrying what look to be firearms clipped to their belts. The small building to the side of the gates has security along the side, indicating that we've hit a checkpoint of sorts. My old school certainly didn't have anything like this, you could drive right through their gates uninterrupted.

Walking in line with their determined strides are two abnormally large, long-coated shepherds, their gaze pinned to our car. I have never seen dogs like them before, with the height of a Great Dane but the appearance of a German Shepherd. They move in perfect sync with their handlers, baring their teeth as they get closer to us.

They're magnificent. The pair lift their noses to the window, causing a small area of fog to appear, their sharp canines on full display. It takes all I have to not jump out of the car and pet them, despite their "all work, no play" demeanor.

The driver lowers his window before handing over the letter my parents had sent with him about my enrollment. Money does incredible things when used correctly, like accepting an arsonist whose only notable skill is preparing a human body for its last viewing. One of the men reads over the letter silently while the other walks around the car with the dog at his heels. His eyes are pinned to the rear seat where I'm sitting, unable to see through the blacked-out windows but knowing I'm there. His hard stare sends a shiver down my spine, a feeling that's not unwelcome.

The man holding the letter gives us a silent nod as the iron gates swing open, revealing a long, winding road that disappears into a mass of towering, scattered oak trees. The woodland is dark and dense, filled with fallen trees and an eerie silence that makes my dark little heart sing. Low-lying fog has settled amongst the bottoms of the trees, adding to the overall allure of this place. Glancing out of the rear window, I see the men and their furry friends standing at attention, watching us disappear into the woods. The whole unexpected situation has me sitting on the edge of the soft leather seat, excited for what will come next.

After ten minutes of sweeping bends and staring at the same dark woods, a clearing finally comes into view, with the centerpiece being one of the most stunning pieces of Gothic architecture that I have ever seen. It looks like a castle had been plucked from medieval Europe with its high-peaked towers and large pointed arches. The entire building is made of light gray stone with intricate details that are hard to see from a distance.

Gargoyles are perched above each side of the entrance, their pointed wing tips looking almost like horns. The stone mouths are open, with pointed fangs and a long, forked tongue snaking out of the small gap. They remind me of some of the books I read, only those gargoyles are usually alive and fucking the female main character. One can only dream.

As the Escalade rolls to a stop, the driver parks and gets out to silently unpack all of my things from the trunk. He drops them at the bottom of the steps and hops back into the car without a word. I collect my things from beside me quickly, opening the door and nearly jumping out to see the building up close.

The sudden chill of the air sends a wave of goosebumps across my legs, my torn tights doing nothing to keep the cold out. The wind howls through the trees and into the clearing, causing my black, pleated skirt to rise above my ass and dance with the breeze. Any attempts to flatten it are futile, with the wind picking it right back up as soon as I move my hands. Luckily, the grounds seem barren, with the only people around being the guards at the front and the driver, who is already in the car with the engine running.

Movement in the entryway catches my eye as a tall, muscular man with disheveled, platinum hair steps out, leaning against the doorway with his arms crossed. His uniform looks scruffy, the black and white tie hanging low on his crumpled, white button-up shirt. One side is roughly tucked into his black slacks, showcasing a silver belt buckle with some form of crest on it. Even though he looks like he just rolled out of bed, this man is hands down one of the most attractive people I have ever set my eyes on.

I attempt to avert my eyes, turning slightly to grasp the handle of one of my suitcases. Usually, I'm able to mask my emotions well, something that was drilled into me at quite a young age. But somehow, this man, without even opening his mouth, has me fighting back a smile as my cheeks start to heat.

"Let me guess, Wynn? The funeral home girl?" He laughs deeply, his lips kicking up into a smirk. Not the most original nickname someone has given me, that's for sure. Is that blood in his hair?

I can feel myself leaning forward slightly to get a better look; the deep crimson is a stark difference to his otherwise almost-white hair. Questions sit on the tip of my tongue, my mind torn between wanting to know more about him and wanting to get as far away from him as possible. The unfamiliar butterflies in my stomach don't seem too put off by the blood nor the danger that flows from the man in front of me.

Glancing around, I still don't see another person in sight other than the Escalade winding its way back down the dark path.

"There looks to be so many of us out here, I don't know how you were able to guess it so easily," I deadpan, dragging my heavy suitcases up the stone steps, the loud clunk echoing through the silence. His chest rises and falls, chuckling as he walks through the timber doors just in time for them to swing back into my face. Mature.

Yanking open the heavy doors, I find him standing close to the doorway, facing me with a smug look on his face. It makes me want to slap the look right off him, almost as much as it draws me in. People are walking through the space behind him, but all of my attention is consumed by the man looking at me with a mischievous glint in his eyes.

I tentatively step forward, feeling the air grow heavier the closer I get to him, like a hand squeezing my lungs and making it hard for me to breathe. His deep, almost red-hued eyes roam down my body, halting at the slashes in my tights before a cruel grin spreads across his face. I have never seen eyes like his before. The color is a beautiful, dark crimson, almost like the color of blood. His eyes meet mine with an intensity that's unfamiliar, charged with emotions that I can't, for the life of me, pinpoint.

His hand reaches into his blazer pocket, pulling out a folded piece of paper and a small black pouch. The moment I take them out of his hands, he steps back, shaking his head. "Here's your key and map, admin circled your room. Classes start tomorrow, the rest you can figure out yourself, I'm sure. Welcome to hell, new girl."

His back is turned before he finishes his sentence, jogging up the large, double staircase and out of sight without a backward glance. For the first time in the last ten minutes, I feel like I can breathe. His presence is unnerving, though that feeling is something I could get used to. It's strange that they sent a student to give me my things, but it's certainly not something I'm going to complain about after that encounter.

Opening up the basic map, I find the mark on the third story in what looks to be a corner room that's separated from the rest. Hauling the suitcases up the stairs, I watch every student pass me in silence, staring in my direction with blank looks on their faces. No smiles, no hellos. Nothing but silence, broken only by my heavy footsteps down the hall and the clicking of my suitcase wheels spinning on the floor. Turning to face them, a smirk tips the corner of my lips. I expect nothing less from a new school, especially one that takes on the caliber of people that this one does. The jokes on them though, I thrive in silence.

Growing up in a funeral home and mortuary, you find comfort in things that others would find uneasy. For me, solace is silence and solitude. Being able to indulge my morbid curiosity without the social pressure. Where other kids would spend their spare time playing sports with their parents, I was taught how to prepare a body for its final viewing. Our family holidays were spent traveling to the other branches of our company, teaching the next generation of mortuary assistants the arts. The scent of embalming fluid still lingers in my nose, strangely bringing a homely feeling to something so clinical. It's always there, acting as a reminder of the place that makes me feel most at ease.

After twenty minutes of navigating the complex inner walls of the academy and being outwardly avoided by every single person I pass, I find my home for the next six months tucked away at the end of a long, quiet hall. The door creaks loudly when I open it, the motion causing a plume of dust to kick up from the floor, making the already dimly lit room look hazy.

Dark timber furniture is spread throughout the space, interlinked with intricate webs that almost sparkle with the small amount of light in the room. I trail a finger along the dusty dresser that's against the wall, leaving a clean line and a thin scratch from my sharp, black stiletto nails behind. My teeth rake along my bottom lip, fighting back the smile that's threatening to crack through. This will be perfect.

The large window draws me in, the ornate design mottling the small amount of light in the room. It looks like a flower at the top, with two peaked panels separated by stone underneath. Thin, black drapes hang from a rail, pooling on the floor. They don't look like they will hold out much light, but it adds to the feel of the room. I drag a chair from the desk setup over to the window and use my sleeve to clean some of the dust from the glass.

My eyes take in the stunning view where the tree line meets the slightly more manicured academy grounds. The low-lying fog settles along the base of the trees like a blanket of mist, making the woods look even more mysterious. I have this feeling in the pit of my stomach that something is watching me, but all I can see is mist, trees, and the looming darkness settling in the sky. Shutting my eyes, I inhale a deep breath before getting to work cleaning up the space.

CHAPTER TWO
WYNN

The old, dusty sheets on the bed are swapped out for my favorite, a deep red silk bed set, the softness dancing across my fingertips as I smooth out the creases. I set out a few of my candles from home, lighting an ambrette wood wick and placing it on the dresser opposite the bed. The crackle from the wood echoes throughout the quiet room, that familiar sound pulling a deep breath from my chest. After a quick clean and adding in some little personal touches and trinkets, the room is much more comfortable than when I first walked in. It's dark, it's secluded, and it's mine.

Padding over to the ensuite, I take in the equally dark space with its mosaic-tiled floor and stone walls. A large shower takes up the corner of the room, with a rain showerhead coming down from the ceiling. Now, this I could get used to.

Switching the faucet to hot, I strip out of my clothes and step into the massive shower, allowing the searing water to cascade down my body, making my skin flush. The sting from the water goes straight to my core, lighting a fire as pain usually does.

My pale skin marks easily, something I have grown to love. There's something about watching the body's reaction to impact and pain that I find fascinating. A fascination that has become something a little...more. The way skin breaks out in chills to both cold weather and featherlight touches, as much as it does when you are aroused, or the way a knife can leave a red mark on the skin until the pressure increases ever so slightly, then it draws blood.

My brain wanders until the water runs cold, which is enough time for the dusk sky to morph into darkness. Slipping into my oversized black tee and panties, I curl into my soft sheets, falling asleep to the soothing sound of rain hitting the window.

My ragged breaths create plumes of white mist in the darkened sky as I search for a safe space to hide. The beast's footsteps fall heavily behind me, its paws breaking the twigs on the forest floor and cutting through the silence. My heart threatens to beat through my chest as it snaps its teeth close to my ear and tears out a few strands of my hair. A yelp escapes me at the sting, causing a growl from the beast.

My senses are overloaded with the cool night air painfully kissing my skin, the sticks and rocks shredding the skin on my bare feet, and the overwhelming smoke that fills my lungs with every inhale.

"Give up, girl," he growls, now beside me as I continue to run, his bright, ember-filled eyes staring straight into mine. I push as hard as I can, the sticks and rocks on the ground tearing into my bare feet and forcing a scream to rip from my throat. My attempt is futile, with the beast simply matching my pace. One swipe of his heavy foot is all it takes to send me tumbling to the ground. I try to break the fall, my hands shooting out in front of my body and catching the brunt of the impact. My hands and knees feel like they have been ripped to shreds from the fall.

He flips my body over, hovering his black, hellish, wolf-like presence above me with a snarl. Smoke pours from his fur as he moves his nose along my collarbone, inhaling deeply. Sticks rip into my skin as I try to shuffle from below him, a futile attempt to escape.

"Don't fucking move, Wynn, this is the only warning that you'll get," he rumbles from above me, his sharp, white teeth glistening in the moonlight. I know I heard him speak, but his lips never moved from the snarl. He looks like something otherworldly, but his being able to speak was not something I was expecting; it was almost like he spoke into my mind somehow. Without warning, his long, black tongue traces along my neck and up to my ear before he nips at my skin, forcing a whimper to escape my lips.

I should be terrified, but instead, I'm drawn to him in a way that I certainly shouldn't be given the situation I find myself in. Heat licks at my core to the point where I can feel wetness drenching my panties. His ember eyes glow brighter on his next inhale as he zones in on the hem of my oversized tee. Surely he can't tell...

"Well, this is a surprise. You're fucking turned on." He chuckles, his entire body shifting into a completely naked man right before my eyes.

My eyes widen as I attempt to take in what in the world just happened. "What the fuck was that?" I breathe out softly, my eyes raking over one of the most dangerous-looking men I have ever laid my eyes on. He's stacked with muscle upon muscle, black and red tattoos covering his body as far as my eyes can see. His black, shaggy hair falls around his face, but it's his eyes that shock me the most. They look like a lit flame is dancing behind his pupils as they bore into mine.

"You need to wake up, little Wynn. Your life just got a whole lot more interesting."

My heart is racing at a speed that feels like it's seconds from bursting through my chest cavity. Taking deep breaths, I rub my thighs together, causing the slightest amount of friction and confirming what I already know. The wetness slowly drips from my core as I stretch my body out, the ache building to an unbearable point. I take a deep breath in, the faint, smokey scent filling my lungs and fueling the burn between my thighs. The memory of the smokey wolf, or man, whatever he was-pinning me to the ground in the woods, forces the need running through my body to intensify.

I delicately run my hand down my curved stomach and into my panties, shimmying them down my thighs for easier access. Closing my eyes, I dip two fingers into my core and slide them back up, drawing circles around my already sensitive clit. The pressure starts to build quickly, as it always does after my nightmares, but something is missing.

Reaching over to the drawer in my nightstand with my other hand, I grasp the sharpened black blade, running the tip along my inner thighs. The pressure is just enough to break the skin as my body sits right on the edge, waiting. Digging the blade in harder, I graze my pointed stiletto nail over my hypersensitive clit, instantly falling apart. My body shakes as my orgasm tears through me violently, releasing the pressure of both the blade and my nail immediately while my body tremors through the aftershocks.

I lay there for a moment, my breath still ragged from the nightmare and the morning self-care session. The rivulets of blood cascade down my thigh, pooling at my discarded panties, which luckily captured most of it. The blade is cleaned with the hem of my tee, and I place it next to my boots so that it's not forgotten for the day.

I pad over to the bathroom, discarding my tee and panties into the small black hamper before stepping into the shower. The scorching hot water runs over my body, washing the blood from my thighs as I watch the trail of pink flowing down the drain. Quickly washing my body, I hop out to patch up the fresh cut. It's not deep, not enough for stitches, but it will definitely add to the existing artwork gracing my body.

For the last few months, my nightmares have taken a turn. I've always had them, even as a child, but lately they've developed into something I don't quite understand. When I wake up, my body is already extremely heightened, and that intense fear lingers, heating my body in a way that nothing and no one else has ever been able to. The figure in my nightmares more recently is dark, towering over my small frame, and threatening my life in one way or another. The situations vary, but all have the same end result. Waking me with a need that only a little pain or fear can fix.

My makeup is done the same as every other day, with a heavy hand on the blush to warm up my pale complexion and a sharp, black-winged liner that could cut a bitch with ease. Unpacking the uniform my parents had purchased before the move, I lay it out across the bed and giggle to myself at just how perfect it is for me with its monochrome tones. The uniform for Blackstone is fitting with its crisp, white shirt; black, plaid skirt that hits slightly above the knee; and my tailored black blazer, which pulls in at my waist, showcasing the dramatic curve of my hips.

Slipping on a pair of torn, black tights and my platform Doc Martens, I straighten my hair until it's a sleek, ink-black curtain hanging down my back and then head out the door. I'm instantly hit in the chest by something covered in blood, and my feet stumble back at the impact as I watch the dead raccoon swaying back and forth on a rope attached to the doorway.

Welcome to Blackstone Academy, Wynn.

CHAPTER THREE
WYNN

My once-white shirt is now covered in the red splatters of blood from my nice little welcome gift this morning. The same blood that is now trickling onto the hallway floor as I make my way to my first class. Having to take the time to cut down my furry friend and actually find my way to the room means that I'm a little bit late.

The halls are barren and silent as I walk to class with the raccoon firmly in my grasp. This part of the building is beautiful, its stone walls lit by hanging pendants and lined with large, arched windows.

I smile sweetly, strolling into the classroom and leaving a trail of crimson in my path. An older lady, who I'm assuming is our teacher, pales at the sight of me. Her warm, brown eyes widen as she takes in my appearance, her angular brows shooting up in shock.

"Hi, Miss, I'm Wynn, but I'm sure you knew that. I was wondering, do you have a lost property bin here? Someone seems to have misplaced their pet roadkill in my doorway this morning," I say confidently, biting back a grin at the look of horror on her face.

I hold up the raccoon, the blood still freely flowing from the tips of its toes into a small pool on the floor. My lip kicks up as I scan the room, seeing most of the students with grossed-out expressions or looking away. A few roll their eyes, sniggering in my direction; one even runs out of the room with her hands over her mouth, and that's when I see them.

Two guys are sitting at the back of the class, looking at me with a burning intensity. One of them is the same one that gave me the map and my warm welcome yesterday. He looks more put together with his platinum-blond hair styled back and the blood now gone. The other is almost a spitting image of the blond, but with black, shaggy hair that falls messily around his face. He seethes, staring straight into my eyes as his incredibly sharp teeth toy with his black lip ring. They both make the desks they are sitting behind look small; their tall, muscular frames are much bigger than the rest of the class.

"Oh look, funeral girl, you made a new friend after all. How nice." The blond twin snorts, his amused gaze never leaving mine. I can hear the low laughs and hushed conversations spreading throughout the room.

Look at the state of her.

Why wouldn't she change first?

Bale is staring at her; he never looks up for that long, unlike his brother.

He looks like he wants to tear her apart.

She won't last long.

From the whispers in the room, I assume that the dark-haired twin's name is Bale, considering that the blond twin had absolutely no qualms about staring me up and down when he welcomed me to the Academy. He's currently staring at me with a kicked-up smirk, in no way looking like he may want to kill me. His brother, on the other hand, his darkness pulls me in. He looks at me with venom in his stare, sparking an ache in my core that I know I can't fix anytime soon.

"I'm assuming that fluffy here belongs to you two?" I laugh, taking confident steps toward the back of the room, stopping between the desks of assholes one and two. Leaning down to their eye level and holding the roadkill with one hand, I reach into my boot and pull the blade out with a wicked smile.

A giggle escapes me as I hear some of the students gasp at the sight of a weapon in the room. You would think they've never seen one before with that sort of reaction. It's not like I'm threatening anyone. Although, if the blond asshole doesn't wipe the smirk off his face, I may need to start.

"I can cut him in half so you don't have to share if you prefer. I have heard twins can get a little jealous if the other has something they don't. For the record, I'm not scared of a dead raccoon, person, or dead anything. Don't waste your time on me, boys. There are plenty of other innocent souls to torture around here that will stroke your fragile ego a little more."

My body is thrumming with a mix of excitement and heat as I stand in wait for some form of reaction from the pair. I bend to tuck the blade back into the side of my boot, only to be caught speechless when I stand back up.

Dark veins start forming below Bale's amber eyes, his obsidian pupils turning into slits right before me. My breathing slows, watching the veins pulse under his skin. I'm standing in a space that blocks him from the view of everyone but his brother, not that he's trying to hide whatever is happening.

"I would step back if I were you, little Wynn. We don't want you murdered on your first day now, do we?" The blond twin's voice rumbles low, stoking the fire already smoldering in my core.

My eyes flick between the two when he speaks, settling back on Bale, who is still staring through my entire fucking soul with an intensity that feels like it will tear me to pieces. It's a dangerous look, one I can see myself getting addicted to quickly.

"Run, little rabbit, as far away from me as you can," Bale growls, his fingers obsessively tapping the desk as the dark veins continue to spread under his skin.

"Wynn, that's enough, please sit down somewhere! Jack, get rid of whatever that thing is and return as soon as possible," the teacher shakily yells from the front of the room. Seconds later, a chair scrapes along the ground, forcing me to turn and look at the boy walking toward me, his eyes zoned in on the creature still dangling in my grip. The poor thing looks like he might throw up the closer he gets, so I make a show of swinging it a little from side to side. Quickly, he takes the roadkill from my outstretched hand and scurries out of the room, leaving a trail of blood in his path.

"Well, that was fun." I laugh, taking the only empty seat in the class, which happens to be directly in front of Bale. A shiver rolls over my entire body as I feel the heat of their stare, forcing my thighs to clench together. Their presence is so dark it's intoxicating, kicking my curiosity into overdrive with a need to know more.

LUKA

My control is slowly slipping, which is not something that Bale and I are used to. I take a deep breath and force my eyes to close as I inhale the scent of the little bitch in front of us. Most people who come too close to us have the scent of fear bleeding from their pores, some curiosity, but mostly fear. Wynn, on the other hand, all I can smell is the sweet scent of her arousal. The excitement and the rush. She isn't scared of us as other humans are, and that's unsettling in itself. Bale and I, as well as the principal, are the only supernatural beings at the academy. The rest of the students and faculty are unaware, or if they aren't, then they're too terrified to say anything, which suits us fine.

Typically, we do not make a show of our other forms or anything else that would give us away, but somehow, this tiny little thing is forcing it out of us like we haven't dealt with this our whole lives. I open my eyes and glance over at Bale, only to find his eyes firmly shut as his fingers tap along his desk in a perfect rhythm. He's sensing her heartbeat, her peaceful, collected heartbeat, and tapping it on the desk to calm himself. I know she saw his eyes change, his form starting to break through. She may not completely understand what it means, but she saw enough to know that Bale isn't completely human.

I turn just in time to see her thighs press together from the side, a quiet gasp escaping her lips that only we would be able to hear. Not that she would know that. She's an absolute vision, and I hate it. It's almost like she was created with us in mind. I would put her at around five feet tall at the most, with curves that make me want to bite into her and mark her all over.

The academy's uniform has never looked like this in the years we have been here; the splattering of blood and her cocky smirk only adding to her beauty. It fits her like a glove, showcasing every dip and curve on her body.

I'm aware of Ms. Archibald attempting to rein in the class and teach us the best she can, but none of her words are making it through to me. My focus is solely on her and the reaction the two of us are having to her presence.

It takes every fiber in my body to not shift right here in the middle of class and take a bite from her thick, tight-clad thighs. My kind are not usually biters, that's more Bale's thing than mine, but I would sell my fucking soul for just a taste.

This is one of those times where I'm glad most of the student population is terrified of us because I have been staring at this girl with zero shame since her ass sat in that seat and those thighs forced themselves together.

Bale still hasn't opened his eyes, his fingers still tapping out her heart rate silently. I watch as his jaw flares while he tenses, the black veins creeping back out from his closed eyes. I kick the side of his desk, jutting my chin toward the door and standing abruptly, the screeching chair causing the whole class to turn and face us.

He looks up at me with glowing, amber eyes before he stands with me, cracking his neck and rolling out his shoulders. His control is slipping quickly, and if I don't get him out of this room right now, they will have to add another fifteen bodies to the school's death count.

Without a word, the pair of us silently stalk out of the room, slamming the door so hard that it snaps from its hinges. Bale walks until he is out of eyeline from the door before kicking up his speed, needing to get out of the halls before anyone sees him.

The two of us are not like others of our kind. Our genetics are unique, having one parent who is a Prince of Hell and the other from the first bloodline of vampires. Where most demons and vampires are created, we were born.

Having grown up dealing with our true forms escaping at inopportune times, we have adapted well. Keeping it under control comes almost naturally to the pair of us, so today has been unexpected, to say the least.

My shoulder blades burn my already heated skin, the black wings fighting with my will to escape. I try to stretch my neck, rolling my shoulders back in an attempt to ease the pain that I know is coming, but it's useless.

The tips slice through my skin as I pick up my pace, running toward her room, knowing that's exactly where he will be. He would have felt the same pull that I did being up close to her and would be craving more of it, only this time without her taunting us.

She doesn't know how thin our control seems to be around her and how dangerous it could be for all of us if that control happens to fucking snap.

CHAPTER FOUR
BALE

B lack, lengthened claws splinter the timber of her desk, the pressure snapping it in two as her laptop and candles tumble onto the floor with a loud thud. Her scent is so strong in here, and yet she has only been here for a day. Imagine the carnage for us both if she stays... My entire body feels like it's on high alert, picking up on every single sound and smell, something I have managed to keep fucking contained for years. I have only just met the girl, and I don't know whether I want to tear her to pieces or bury myself inside her wet cunt while I feast on her pretty little neck.

My combat boots fall heavy on the floor as I storm over to her dresser, ripping the drawers from the rollers one by one to find the source of the pull I'm feeling. There's something here thats drawing me in and feeding the monster that I'm trying my best to contain.

The scent of her blood burns my nose as I get to the last drawer, finding her panties. They're folded perfectly, a range of lace and cotton in shades of red and black. I curl my hand around them, bringing a handful up to my nose and inhaling deeply, a low growl escaping my throat at the scent. They smell of washing powder and blood, mixed with the sweet scent of her. The panties are completely clean, but my senses are always heightened being what I am. Even more so when my body is on alert like this, which isn't often anymore.

I collect all her panties from the drawer, filling my blazer pockets to the brim, partially to teach the little bitch a lesson but also because it means I can take the scent of her with me. Just as the last pair hits my pocket, Luka appears in the doorway, his eyes wide and red.

"What the fuck did you do, Bale?" he yells, storming into the space and taking in the carnage. His blazer is torn along his back, with two large, pointed wing tips ripping through the material. She's affecting him just as much as she is affecting me.

"He was right, wasn't he? About her?" I growl, my claw fidgeting with a bit of lace in my pocket carefully. It's not like I don't have enough money to replace them if I tear them to shreds, but I don't want to rip them all. Not just yet anyway.

Luka paces the length of her room, balling his hands into fists before releasing his grip and going again. His heart rate begins to slow back to a normal rate within minutes before he turns to me and nods.

"Let's get out and call Dad. He would know, and if he doesn't, one of the princes surely would," Luka says calmly, turning on his heel and leaving the room as quickly as he can with his wings tucked tightly behind him.

We need to make her leave Blackstone as soon as possible. Luka and I are here for a purpose, a protection order from our father to the school. The last thing we need is to not have any control over ourselves.

If his prediction is correct and this puny little human is our mate, we will break her, and that has the potential to ruin both of us. There is lore about angels being able to be with humans safely, but not for our kinds. If she stays, she risks not only the very reason we were put here but us in general, and I'm not letting her fuck our lives up like that.

Our father built the Academy over four hundred years ago to sit right over Hell's gates. At the time, it was a ruse, a cover for the gates, and a place to stay if he was needed here on this plane. Over the years, suspicion rose about the property in the middle of the woods after hunters and hikers found it on their travels.

He, along with the other princes, decided that it would become Blackstone Academy. A school for the criminals, the outcasts, and the pretty little bitches who burn their entire school to the ground apparently. The space is large enough to be overseen by humans easily, and at least one demon would be able to integrate into the school to keep watch. It had been quiet for years, until now.

"Dad is coming to visit anyway, to check on how we're doing," Luka growls from ahead, sounding pissed. "As for our little Wynn issue, he started rambling about all that fate bullshit again, so he is absolutely no help. I say we run her out, scare her off a little. She wouldn't survive the bond between the three of us anyway, being human. We can't have her here if our control is going to slip like this, or we will end up back down in the rings with Dad."

I nod in agreement, ideas flooding through my mind of the fun we could have with this, with her, before we run her out for good.

The two of us storm down the hall, ignoring the stares from the students parting to let us walk through. We need to get back to our wing and plan some of this out before our father gets here, or we are in a world of shit that I would rather not be in. I thrive in chaos, but the Ring of Wrath that we call home is not the place for a vampire. At least, not for me.

If it wasn't for the bond I have with Luka, I would have escaped Hell or died trying well before now. Fucked off just like my mom had, as far away from Hell as I could get. I have tried to run, to flee from the shit. I always ended up going back because, as much as he pisses me off, Luka is a part of me with the whole twin bond thing.

Being separated for periods of time physically hurts the both of us, so after a few failed attempts, I stayed and put up with the torment of being the 'bad twin' in Hell with our tyrant of a father. Being one of two born sons of Satan came with big expectations, none of which I could live up to based purely on the fact that I was born a vampire and not a demon.

A large figure stops me in my tracks, tearing me from my thoughts as I slam into him mid-stride. "Boys, I think we need to have a chat. Now!" Headmaster Pierce orders, nodding down the hall toward his office. I don't move, crossing my arms over my chest and raising a brow at Pierce.

Luka laughs off to the side, jumping up to sit on a display table along the wall with his legs swinging gleefully. "Grab your popcorn, boys and girls, the show is about to begin." He grins, settling into his spot with a smirk plastered across his face. Asshole.

Students start flowing into the hall, some taking out their cameras and facing them my way while the others whisper in hushed tones.

What does Pierce think he's doing? Bale's a psycho.

Did you see how he stormed out earlier?

He looks so fucking hot when he's mad.

I try to hold back a chuckle, my sharp teeth raking over my bottom lip and drawing the smallest amount of blood. Part of me says to stop them, snap their phones into pieces, and leave. Father would likely get pissed at me for letting this scene play out and take it out on me. The other part of me doesn't give a flying fuck. My eyes turn back to the waste of space in front of me, his feigned authority starting to dwindle right before my eyes.

His already pale skin lightens, showing me the pulsing blue veins cording up his neck as he takes a step back from me, trying to put some distance between us. It's cute that he thinks that will do anything to change what's happening. He started this, not us.

"You are just like your father. Luka, stop messing around and get down. You are making a scene," Pierce calls out, his nostrils flaring in anger and his shoulders starting to tremble. "I don't want to make a scene, there are students. Come on, let's just go to the office where we can have a chat."

"Get the stick out of your ass, Pierce. What do you fucking need?" I seethe, my patience for the man they have taking care of this place starting to wear thin. With us attending, they didn't see the use in having a demon running the academy like usual, and this jackass managed to weasel his way in. He's a banished angel, stripped of any and all power and ability. At this point, he may as well be a human, just without the use of being a food source for our kind.

Angels, especially fallen angels, are nasty little fucks. They are bitter creatures that have no purpose and no true home to go to. Add this to the fact that we are literally the spawn of Satan, and you have yourself an angry little angel. One whose shit I'm not willing to put up with.

Still standing in front of Pierce, I push forward, backing him into the wall opposite Luka and caging him in place between my arms. His dull, brown eyes widen as he trips on his own feet while stumbling back, bracing himself on my arms to hold him up.

"Y—you need to stop making these scenes in front of the students," he stutters, his eyes blinking rapidly as he stares into mine. With my back to the students, I let a little of my vampire side slip through, the black veins spreading under my now-glowing, amber eyes. "Ri—ripping doors off hinges and hanging dead animals up in the hall is too much. The bad press is already too much, and we can't draw attention like that," he all but whispers, his heartbeat racing a million miles an hour by the end of his little speech.

My body can sense her before I see her, the dark figure stepping into the corners of my vision. The overwhelming ambrette scent mixes with a faint hint of her blood, forcing my eyes away from Pierce's to zone in on her.

She stands at the front of the crowd, watching the exchange curiously, her eyes flitting between me and Luka, whose glee has already shifted to something much more intense. His shoulders roll back, which I'm assuming is to try and stop his wings from slicing through his skin as they had earlier. They tend to get a little trigger-happy when his emotions are heightened, one of the few things that he finds harder to control.

Her eyes travel slowly down my body, halting at my arms that are still caging in Pierce. Her tongue slides along her lower lip before her teeth bite down on the soft, pink flesh. She catches me staring at her intensely, a cocky grin spreading across her lips while she turns and walks toward the crowd. She strolls away with a sway in her hips through the students, whose eyes are flitting between the two of us.

Her attitude makes me want to tear her throat out as much as it makes me want to pin her down and fuck it right out of her. She should be scared of us, even just a little, but instead, the girl gets fucking wet.

"Bale, back to Pierce, focus," Luka whispers. His words are low enough that only I'm able to hear him with my heightened hearing, and other students would be none the wiser.

I look over at him briefly, seeing the way he is gripping the table beneath him so hard that it's starting to splinter.

One of my hands dives into the pocket of my blazer, grabbing hold of a piece of lace and running it through my fingers, while the other remains beside Pierce's head. The darkness slowly recedes with the feeling of the soft material against my rough fingertips.

"I dare you to fucking try. You're forgetting your place here, Pierce," I snarl, turning back to face the now-shivering head-master, who is nodding frantically as he watches the darkness start to spread throughout my veins.

He slips under my arm, running off to his office while muttering words he knows only we will hear. "I hope your father puts you little assholes ba–back in your box when he gets here."

I can smell the smoke before I turn and see Pyro standing there in the flesh. He's crazy for walking inside the academy grounds, knowing that we're hunting his kind. Fire mutts typically wouldn't be stupid enough to walk into a space like this unless they were prepared to tear the place to shreds with everyone in it. This asshole, on the other hand, walks into the space in his more human form, if you could call it that.

Luka jumps down from the display table, walking to stand beside me with his arms crossed across his chest, blocking him from the students who are scurrying around us. The hall quickly starts to empty, the students bustling to get out of the space as quickly as they can. They're used to the altercations with Peirce, but Pyro? I can understand the mass exodus. He looks out of place in these halls, standing at almost seven feet and covered head to toe in tattoos.

He elicits fear in humans by his presence alone, which is one of the things that hellhounds are known for. They can then siphon the fear and feed themselves just by walking into a space with people.

"You're testing limits by stepping foot inside this place, Pyro. Especially after the shit your puppy pals have been causing," I rumble, preparing myself to launch at him if needed. I would have thought he would be in his demon form if he were here to fight us, but you never know with these sly assholes. My muscles begin to tense as I let my vamp out to play, itching to be able to tear off a slice of him after the day I've had.

He walks toward us from the entryway, smoke lingering around him with each confident step he takes until he's within arm's reach. A cruel smirk spreads across his face as the fire in his eyes burns a little brighter. "Aw, not happy to see me, boys?" He grins, his lengthened canines on full display.

"Just get to the fucking point, fluffy, I'm starving." Luka laughs and rolls his eyes at the maniac standing in front of us.

"Your little...mate. You need to...oh, I don't know, actually keep her safe. There will be more of us coming, and they want her, fucking dead or alive," he snaps, the laugh having fallen from Pyro's face as soon as he spoke about her. His eyes harden, his focus moving from one of us to the other with an intensity that I wasn't expecting. "Fail this, and I will tear your throats out myself and feed your meat suits to the bottom feeders." Without another word, he turns and strides out of the hallway, slamming the door on his way out.

The hellhounds sent before him were grunts, lowly demons who wanted to get in the good graces with one of the princes. Pyro is different from the usual grunts and is known throughout Hell as one of the best enforcers. Our father has even used him from time to time, and he avoids the use of other demons as much as possible. Considering he is one himself, he doesn't trust many of them. Why would an enforcer want to keep the girl safe?

Part of me wishes he had stayed to cause a bit more of a scene; I could have used the outlet to get rid of some of this pent-up rage that's itching to escape. Luka claps once loudly beside me, his ability to shift from one emotion to the next is something I certainly do not possess. He could be covered head to toe in blood with a dead angel at his feet one moment and unbothered while laughing at his own joke the next. Me, on the other hand, I'm the opposite.

"Well, that was weird. Okay, here's the plan; cafeteria first because I need to siphon something that isn't dead inside like your grumpy ass. Then, back to the wing to figure this shit out because things just got a lot more complicated with Pyro somehow being involved." Luka laughs, walking toward the cafeteria.

CHAPTER FIVE
WYNN

I walk into the cafeteria, although it feels wrong to describe this room as something so mundane. The hall is large, with high, domed ceilings and light, stone-covered walls. All of the tables in the space look like light-colored marble with the sun hitting them beautifully through the tall, arched windows.

The lunchtime rush seems to be in full swing, with people attempting to bustle past me, only to see my bloodstained clothes and turn in the opposite direction with a look of disgust plastered across their faces. You would think an academy with the caliber of students that Blackstone has, that they wouldn't shy away from a little blood. But everyone seems to be avoiding me like the plague.

An audible chuckle escapes me as one poor girl's face pales to the lightest pink hue I have ever seen. Her eyes are as wide as saucers while she holds her breath, taking in the sight of me.

"It's okay. He didn't suffer. I don't think he did anyway. Actually, maybe ask the twins," I say with a laugh, looking down at my blood-covered white shirt, before leaving her frozen in her place to join the rapidly building food line.

Quickly getting a sandwich and a black coffee, I find one of the only vacant tables, but as soon as my ass hits the seat, a loud whistle sounds from a few tables over. My eyes zone in on the two of them sitting at a table by themselves, both polar opposites and yet so similar at the same time.

Smiling sweetly, I stare straight into the blond brother's eyes and flip my middle finger up before taking a bite of my lunch. His gaze drops to my mouth, watching intently as I take each bite. His eyes feel like they are devouring my soul; a heavy pull from the pit of my stomach increasing every time I risk a glance at him.

I chance a look at Bale, who is staring at something in his lap with a scowl while one of his large, tattooed hands taps the tabletop in a steady rhythm that seems to gain momentum the longer my eyes linger. He's intense, and without even looking my way, I can feel his darkness rolling over me, forcing goosebumps to form across my skin.

Shifting my focus, I look down at my half-eaten sandwich and open my mouth to take a bite just as a shiver spreads across my body and the tiny hairs on the back of my neck stand on end.

"Do you need a lesson on personal space?" I deadpan, dropping my food onto the plate in front of me. A low rumble sounds from behind me, but there's no response other than the cackle coming from the direction of the twin's table and the general bustle of students surrounding us. "Not much of a talker? It's Bale, right?" I laugh, picking up my sandwich and taking another bite without turning to face him. He chuckles before bringing himself down to my level, his face now parallel with mine. I drop my food once more when I feel his cool breath on my skin with each laugh, forcing a shiver to run up my spine.

"Don't bother learning names, funeral girl, you'll be gone before the end of the day," he all but growls, the deep, gravelly tone stoking the heat already building in my core from his presence alone. His face dips lower, lips ghosting along my neck, and halting at my pulse point where he nips at the skin lightly. My body betrays me as I lean in closer to chase that little sting before I have a chance to stop myself.

I look around, remembering that we are in a space filled with people, only to find the room completely empty. Well, almost empty. Still sitting back in his chair with a cocky grin plastered on his painfully handsome face is Bale's twin. He's kicking back, enjoying the show with his muscular arms crossed over his chest and his feet up on the table.

"The raccoon was a good one, I'll give you that, but come on. Surely you've figured out I'm not rattled by your shit after this morning. You don't look stupid, at least not much anyway," I say with a grin, rising from my chair and spinning around to face him as he straightens back up, once again towering over me.

Anger rolls off of him in waves as I watch his eyes start to spin black veins like they did this morning. His jaw flares, staring into my eyes while I watch the veins spread, tracing beautiful, lightning-like patterns under his skin.

I had considered in class that this may have been a trick of the light, my eyes not adjusting correctly or something. But here, for the second time today, I can see them clear as day. Bale isn't human, at least not entirely, and I need to know more.

Without thinking, I reach up and delicately trace one of the veins from his undereye to his cheek. His skin is cool to the touch, almost like he had been in the mortuary chamber, but he's alive and breathing, and looking at me with a pained expression. He closes his eyes and leans slightly into my touch, his hand reaching up to cover mine as I run my fingers along his cheek. I wonder if it hurts when the veins spread like this?

I'm suddenly ripped from Bale and spun around, ending up face-to-face with his twin. My hands fly out and grip his arms tight to avoid falling, his biceps instantly tensing under my fingers while his hold on my shoulders remains firm. The blond twin's eyes are menacing-a deep red hue surrounding the darkest, jet-black pupils I have ever seen. Unless he is wearing contacts, he can't be human either with eyes like this.

"Could you please, for the love of all that is holy, steer clear of him?" He snarls, nodding toward the hulkingly huge figure slamming the doors to the cafeteria on his way out, snapping them off the hinges just like he had earlier in class.

My hand snakes down his arm, eyes staring into his to try and keep his focus, while I dig my stiletto nails into his hand as hard as I can, a failed attempt to loosen his grip on my shoulders.

"Keep him on a tighter leash, and we won't have any issues, blond twin. Last I checked, the asshole walked up to me, not the other way around." I bite back sweetly, the blood from my nails digging into his skin now dripping down my wrist, a cascading trail staining my skin crimson in its path. His eyes remain locked on mine with no signs of pain or discomfort, the intensity of his stare shifting from anger to amusement within seconds.

The heat flowing through my core is almost painful at this point, aching for a little hint of pressure. My thighs instinctively rub together in an attempt to relieve some of the pain before a growl rips me from my lust-filled thoughts.

His raised brow and cocky smirk are enough to tell me he not only saw my thighs rubbing together, but he understood why I did it.

"Ahh, so our little mate does get turned on by our presence."

"What the fuck do you mean by mate? We're far from friends. I have only just gotten here, and you've been a prick since I stepped foot on Blackstone Academy grounds," I snap, digging my nails into his skin harder, but he doesn't flinch.

His eyes flit over to my wrist, intently watching as his blood disappears under the cuff of my blazer. He breathes in deeply, closing his eyes momentarily before leaning in closer, his face now inches from mine. We're both silent for a moment, his nearness searing my skin to an almost unbearable point, unlike his twin. Where Bale's skin feels cold to the touch, Luka's is almost like warming your hand near an open flame. Both extremities are painful, but in a way that draws me in and leaves me wanting more.

His grip on my shoulder releases as he closes the small amount of distance that is between us, looking down at me like he wants to devour me whole. I should run. Take this moment to get away from him and get back to my room, but I don't. Instead, I stand there, drawn to him, curious to know more.

"Firstly, my name is Luka, so cut the blond twin bullshit. Secondly, tell me, Wynn, what is it about me and my brother that makes your cunt so fucking wet? Have you thought about the reaction you have to us and why you have it, or did you just think it was because we are hot as fuck?" He asks, raking his perfectly white teeth over his lip as though he is biting back a laugh.

"You two couldn't make anyone wet if your lives depended on it." I smile, jumping as Luka's bloodied hand wraps around the column of my throat, squeezing the sides slightly. My grin drops as I feel my arousal coating my inner thighs while I squirm in his hold.

"Is that so? Because I can fucking smell you, Wynn. We're going to have so much fun together, just you wait."

PYRO

I should have killed her. I should have killed her or taken her just like I was tasked to. Instead, instinct made me enter her dream and chase her like the perfect piece of prey she is. The image of her running with those thick, bare thighs on full display is seared into my mind, and I can't for the life of me get it out. The way her body felt under mine in my hellhound form, so fragile and breakable... Fuck.

The asshole twins are the two watching over the Academy at the moment, alongside the waste of space fallen angel, who may as well not be here, so this girl is nowhere near safe. As much as I need to go back home and figure out why I can't seem to kill her, the pull to protect the girl I'm supposed to be killing is much stronger.

My kind are fairly solitary, unlike the fleabag shifters that people mistake us for. We were made for one purpose and one purpose only, which I just so happen to excel at. To kill. Angels, demons, gods even. Whatever we're ordered to kill, we do. My kind can collect souls, something I've been tasked with before, and can shift between our demon form and human-like form at will.

I lean against the wall in the hallway, waiting until I see her storm around the corner with a scowl plastered across her hauntingly beautiful face. She looks fucking stunning; the blood splatter all over her shirt somehow makes her even more delectable. She halts suddenly, her eyes widening at the sight of me while her full, pink lips purse together.

"Little Wynn." I give her a nod, my voice gravelly from the smoke coursing through me.

My words seem to knock her out of her shock because her arms cross against her ample chest as her eyes roam over my body from head to toe. She's confident, not attempting to hide her perusal of me in any way. I don't move a muscle, soaking in the attention like a man starved.

"Hmm, so you are real, dog boy?" She smirks, her heart rate gaining speed while she watches the fire in my eyes flicker. She must remember me from her nightmare last night. Interesting.

"My name is Pyro," I respond, biting back a laugh at how cute defiance looks on her. She drops her arms from her chest and walks closer, her eyes staring into mine in a way that feels like she's looking directly into my soul, or lack thereof.

"Well, Pyro, what're you doing outside my room? I have dealt with enough assholes today, and my patience is low."

I grab her shoulders and spin her so her back is to the wall before pushing her into it with force. My arms cage her in, bracing the wall on either side of her face while I watch her attempt to regain her composure. Her eyes close for a moment while she pulls in deep breaths, centering herself before looking up at me with those ice-blue eyes. The pull I have toward this girl is so strong, as if it's physical, like my body craves to be close to hers.

In all my years, this has never happened, a pull like this toward another being. The strong need to protect her. To fuck her. To breed her. I didn't think it was possible, but coming face-to-face with her in the flesh like this and having her body so goddamn close to mine... There is no doubt in my mind, she is fated not only to those little pricks but to me too.

I lean in, inhaling her sweet scent, the mix of Wynn herself and the lust pouring from her, forcing my cock to thicken in my jeans. The barbells rub painfully against the zipper with each movement, and the fire burning through my veins gets warmer by the second.

"You need to stay out of the woods, and preferably inside the walls of the Academy. You're a defiant little thing, I can see that clear as day, but for fuck's sake, please just listen," I growl out, my control over my hellhound form slowly slipping.

"I have somehow managed to see you in a dream. Once. Why the fuck would I listen to someone I have never actually met? Now, Pyro, leave before I slice my blade across that pretty fire tattoo you have on your throat and watch you bleed to death." She laughs before ducking under my arms and into her room, slamming her door once she's inside.

Attempting to take deep breaths, I storm down the hall, my combat boots falling heavy on the timber floors. The need to get back into the woods and shift is burning through me like a fire licking at the surface of my skin, threatening to rip right through it.

As soon as my feet hit the dirt, my hellhound form takes over, lighting my entire body on fire and morphing into my more primal state. I take off across the clearing and into the woods, finding my prime position to watch over her through her window.

CHAPTER SIX
WYNN

I lock the door quickly and fall back against it before taking in the carnage in front of me. Clothes are strewn across every surface with claw marks marring the timber furniture, and my desk has been completely broken in two, with my laptop in pieces on the floor below it covered in glass and wax from my favorite candle.

My hand skates along the claw marks on my dresser, sinking into the deep gauge and sending a shiver down my spine. It looks like an animal has torn through my room, but my gut feeling is telling me something different. It's almost like I can still feel their presence here, regardless of the fact that I'm completely alone, and that thought excites the hell out of me.

Making a start on cleaning the space for the second day in a row, I slowly pick up each article of clothing off the floor, finding slashes in some of the things I have worn most recently. Within half an hour, the dresser is put back together, and all the clothes that do not need to be fixed or cleaned are neatly packed away.

All except my panties.

Every single pair that I own is missing, nowhere to be found, solidifying that this wasn't an animal ripping through my room. Well, at least, I don't think they are animals of any kind. My mind has been buzzing thinking of what they could be. Based on the books and movies, both of them are something supernatural, but what exactly, I don't know.

I want to be mad, I want to hope I can rip whoever took them to pieces, and I want to think they should be begging for the mercy of my blade slicing along their corded throats, but I don't. As I look around at the utter destruction of my room, my body feels more alive than it has in years.

Walking over to the window, I take in the beautiful view. The sky is a dusky orange and grows darker by the second as the last of the light disappears. The dense woodland has already started to spread a fine mist along the forest floor, creeping out into the clearing between the school and the trees. Out of the corner of my eye, I see a faint blue glow in the darkness.

It takes all of me to not put on a coat and walk down there to see what it is, but after the day I've had, it's probably best to try and rest rather than put my life on the line traipsing through a dark forest where God knows what's lurking in the shadows.

Luka, Bale, and Pyro have very distinctly colored eyes, with none of them being blue or cool-toned in the slightest. I want to know more about the three of them, to push their buttons a little to see if they snap, they draw me in. Their darkness pulls at the dark little parts of my soul, but even I have some self-preservation, and going down there after a warning like I just had seems like a death wish.

PYRO

I stalk along the tree line in my hellhound form, my heavy feet snapping the branches with every step and echoing throughout the quiet woods. After tearing through the clearing earlier, I had almost expected a visit from the twins. I'm glad when I don't see them because I don't have time for their bullshit tonight when I can sense there is another of my kind out here.

It's hard to be agile when you're the size of a grizzly bear and lit on fire from the inside out. Smoke pours from my fur with every step, hitting the cool mist that covers the forest floor and mixing together, creating white, swirled patterns in the night air.

I pad closer to the edge of the clearing once I see her shadow moving behind the thin, black curtain of her window. I watch as her curvy little body leans down to blow out her candle before she hops into bed.

The memory of her sweet ambrette scent sends a shiver down my spine; the need to be closer to her winning out against attempting to talk to the assholes yet again.

Before I'm able to enter her dream, a twig snaps from behind me. My body whips around to face whoever it is–another hellhound out to hunt the trio. "Lucian," I snarl, baring my teeth.

He's smaller than me and has a ragged, dull charcoal coat that's blurred by his blackened smoke. I roll my shoulders back, preempting the fight that will likely be thrown my way. Lucian is a lowly hellhound, but he's scrappy, and I don't have the time to be out here injured and trying to heal while she's at risk.

"He knew you couldn't do it, Pyro. This was all a fucking test, and you failed," he snaps, his blue eyes getting brighter and releasing glowing embers into the mist. "He's calling you off the job. Report back now or you will be another name on the hit list."

Lev had been acting strange when he gave me this mission. He's the keeper of Hell's gate, the Prince of Envy, and he lives up to his sin in every way possible. I'm one of his best hunters, guarding the gate for the last 200 years. Collecting souls, severing heads, whatever was needed, I did it regardless of whether I agreed. Well, until now.

My ear twitches when the sound of a cry comes from her room, assaulting my senses one by one. The fear coming from her is intoxicating, even at a distance. Now is not the fucking time, Wynn.

"Mmmmmm, she smells...delectable, Pyro. It's a shame they would never share her with you, isn't it? You won't always be around to protect her, and devil knows those idiots don't seem to understand what she is to them." He laughs before running deeper into the woods and out of sight in seconds.

I'm torn between chasing after him or getting to her to help her through the nightmare, but the terrified scream coming from her room makes my decision for me. He had come to send me back, but I'm not leaving her in the twin's incapable hands.

Shifting into my human form, I race to the entrance at the side of the building just as a loud howl in the distance hurries my movement, the need to get to her building by the second.

Forcing my shadows out to unlock the side door, I tiptoe through the halls, hearing her cries getting louder with each step I take. My shadows flow into the lock, clicking the mechanism, and swinging the door open with a thud. As soon as I step through the doorway, the door is quietly shut behind me and locked. Not that it would really keep anyone out. She doesn't move an inch, her body exposed on her bed against the moonlight pouring into the room.

The entire space has been torn to shreds, claw marks slashing across almost every timber surface. Her body starts to writhe, a light cry escaping her lips as her body curls into itself against the sheets.

I stalk over, unable to enter her nightmare once it has already started. While I can't join her, I can keep her in a lucid state so she doesn't wake with a fright. Benefits of being a hellhound.

Her thighs rub against each other with force while her hips buck off the mattress, her pained expression tempting the hound clawing inside me to escape once more. My hands glide from her ankles to her thighs, surprising me when she instinctively parts her thighs at my touch. The scent of her arousal assaults my senses, my breathing becoming labored at the display right in front of me.

She isn't wearing any fucking panties.

I lean in close, her scent drawing me in. I should resist, but I am a demon, after all, and there's only so much I can take before I selfishly snap. Lifting her tee up to expose her just a little more, I see the scars lining her thighs, one so fresh that a rivulet of blood cascades down her pale thigh and disappears into the red sheets. My tongue flattens against the stream, licking until I reach the wound.

Her hips buck, seeking the warmth from my tongue as I lick a trail along her scarred thighs. I sensed what she did that first morning after her nightmare with me, the way she cut her thighs to find her release. I could heal her if I was in my hellhound form, but the blood looks too fucking delectable against her skin.

Footsteps sound from outside her door, pacing up and down the hall. The sound of claws digging into the timber door pulls me from her, her hips raising to chase the heat.

"I can hear you in there, mutt," Bale growls from behind the door, his voice deep and laced with pure rage. "Get the fuck away from her before I tear in there and rip your spine out of your ass and drain you fucking dry."

He's known for his manic temper, the anger always simmering under the surface, seconds from erupting. He's similar to me, not that I would ever admit it to that growly asshole.

"You come in here in that state, and you'll kill her Bale. She has nightmares, and she won't live through the night if you step a fucking foot in here," I snarl, causing her to jump in her sleep.

"Why would you give a single, flying fuck about what happens to the girl?" He yells, slamming something into the other side of the wall. Luckily, her room is in one of the older wings of the place, with barely any other students down this far.

"If I wanted her dead, Bale, she would already be in pieces and not laying here needing a release to calm the fuck down." My body is braced on the bed between her legs, waiting to see how this plays out. He could rip through the door at any moment, but for some reason, he hasn't, not yet anyway.

He doesn't move from outside the door, a loud thud echoing throughout the room as he more than likely drops to the floor. His fingers tap at the door in perfect sync with her rapid heart rate while I settle back between her thighs.

A loud moan rips from her throat as I glide my tongue up to her clit, flicking the sensitive little thing while my fingers ease into her pussy. My canines start to descend, sitting on either side of her clit as my fingers curl inside of her, causing her to tighten around me.

A growl escapes my throat at the thought of fucking her and how tight she would feel around my cock. How my knot would push her perfect cunt to its limits and hold my cum inside her. The need to fill her, to breed her, is overwhelming. My cock is as hard as stone as I grind it against the soft bedsheets, while my tongue devours her whole. I can feel her body start to tremble, her walls clamping down around my fingers with a vice-like grip.

Wrapping my free hand around my length, I glide my grip along the row of barbells tightly, sending the sweet sting of pain straight through my body as I run over each piercing. Her screams fill the room as her release covers my face, dripping onto the sheets below us. Holy fucking shit!

My cock hardens unbearably, chasing its own release while my tongue continues to flick against her core, because fuck knows if I'll ever get the chance to taste her again. My knot starts to swell painfully in my hand, thickening with each movement I make until my tongue ghosts over her clit once more. She whimpers, her body continuing to shake under my hold. The sound is what finally sends me over the edge as I cum on the sheets beneath me.

The need to mark her is strong as I swipe through my release, coating my hands before touching her. Reaching up, I run my fingers along her sensitive pussy, gliding two of my fingers inside her core, marking her with my scent.

"Was that really fucking necessary, Pyro?" Bale seethes through the door before storming off down the hall, pushing things over on his way past. I can only imagine the destruction students are going to wake up to tomorrow after his tantrum.

Her body turns over, goosebumps scattering along her pale thighs from the cool air. She seems relaxed, her breathing evening back out, and her heart rate going back to a normal rhythm. I cover her with the comforter, wrapping it tightly around her shoulders, before shifting back to my hellhound form to warm up the space with my presence. The heat in the room picks up quickly with me curled up in the corner, watching over her.

CHAPTER SEVEN

BALE

P ushing through the door to our wing, I storm inside, slamming the door behind me.

"Well, well, well. Look what the cat dragged in. It's Mr. I-am-going-to-treat-her-like-I-hate-her-but-then-check -on-her-while-she-sleeps," Luka taunts from the lounge as he tosses his gaming controller onto the plush, black sofa beside him. All of the lights in the space are dimmed, casting most of the room in darkness, just as I had left it.

"Now isn't the time, asshole," I snarl, stalking toward my room to avoid this conversation, or at least try to.

"Not so fast, come on. Did you break in and watch her sleep? Sit in the dark like a creep while our pretty little thing slept soundly without a care in the world?" He calls out, switching off the television and following behind me.

"No. She came all over Pyro, from what I could hear. He kept her lucid and made her come during a nightmare. Her fuck-ing whimpers, Luka…" I trail off, flinging my bedroom door open and walking toward the black wingback chair in the corner.

Luka rushes forward, pushing me against the closest wall with his hand around my throat and his eyes hazy, the dark swirls taking over the red in his pupils.

"What the fuck? Can you repeat that because I can't have heard that right?" He orders, giving me a death glare like he's about to rip right through me. To be honest, I wouldn't mind the fight with him tonight. After the day we had, we could both let off some steam.

"As I said, she was having a nightmare, and Pyro was in her room. He made her come, then marked her cunt with his scent. Need more details?" I snap back, pulling his arm from my throat and pushing past him, throwing my shoulder into his with force. Walking over to the chair, I let my body fall into it, leaning my head back into the backrest.

"After spending the day with her today, feeling her skin, seeing how she reacts to us, I don't think I can let her go like we planned, Bale," he huffs, dropping into the chair opposite mine.

"It's too dangerous, Luka. You know that as well as I do. Show some restraint and stop thinking with your cock," I respond, not bothering to look at him, my head still tipped back. "We need to stick to the plan, no matter how tempting it is to give in. Stick to the fucking plan."

"That could've been us, you know. We could have been tasting her. Sharing her," Luka snarls, extending his wings dramatically before tucking them behind him, giving the illusion of two horns on each side of his head. "A fire mutt has tasted what is rightfully ours before we even got close."

He storms out of the room, slamming the door shut on his way out. Knowing my brother, he will be fine in the morning, but he will want to pay the girl a visit to check on her.

For me, being close to her is a fucking danger. The pull I feel is so strong that it causes me pain to be away from her, but whenever we're close, it takes all I have to control myself. If I were to lose that control, I don't know whether that would result in her being torn to pieces or not having a choice with a mating bond.

What makes it worse is that she seems to thrive on my struggle. She likes to push me to see how far she can take it. The girl sees my anger, my true form escaping, and she gets so wet that it starts to drip down her thighs. She tempts my beast, and he's more than happy to give her what she craves.

WYNN

As usual, I wake with a jolt just as the sun starts to rise and fills the room with a muted orange light. I stretch out my body, the muscles light and relaxed, and the usual ache after a night of nightmares missing. My hands trace the soft, damp sheets below me at the realization.

He was here. I thought I had felt him, but my body wasn't quite asleep nor awake. All I know is that I felt something. Something I couldn't easily explain.

My fingers ghost across my core, spreading myself apart to feel where the twinge of pain is coming from. I can feel two cuts on either side of my clit, and when I pull them up, I find my fingers coated in fresh blood. Well fuck, that's hot as all freaking sin.

My eyes adjust to the morning light as a thick layer of smoke lingers along the ceiling, filling my lungs with every breath. It smells like a campfire has been lit in the room, the burning embers tickling my nose. My mind goes back to the nightmare where I first met Pryo, the smokey, wolf-like creature smelt almost exactly the same as my room. He must have been here but not as a person, and I slept through the whole damn thing.

I shower quickly, dressing in a short, black denim skirt with fishnets and black, lace-topped socks. I rustle through the tops in my drawer, finding a grey and black striped sweater before buckling on a black leather under-bust harness. It's the weekend, so I may as well look a little more like myself.

I brush a dusting of amber across my lids with a sharp winged liner and a red-tinted gloss for my lips. A smirk spreads across my face as I walk out of the door, the air hitting between my thighs with each step.

Waiting just outside my door are the twins, both casually leaning against the wall with their hands in their pockets. Standing next to each other, they are a force.

Bale looks good enough to fucking eat, with his black, ripped jeans and combat boots; his black t-shirt with 'mayhem' written across the chest; showcasing the tattoos sprawling up his arms and neck. Even just being in their presence wakes up my body, which already feels like it has been on high alert since I stepped foot onto Blackstone turf.

Luka's a little more subdued, dressed in light denim jeans and a white t-shirt. They are two polar opposites standing side by side. My mind goes back to yesterday, remembering the feeling of Bale's teeth on my neck and his twin's hands around my throat. I giggle as I feel my core tighten at the memory, remembering exactly how it felt after that run-in.

"Oh look, it's my mates." I smile at the twins, using air quotes at the word mates. "What a pleasant surprise on a Saturday morning."

Bale's nostrils flare, his heated eyes raking over my body from head to toe and back up again. His stare pins me in place, and I'm unable to move even if I wanted to.

Luka breaks the silence, striding confidently toward me, his hand ghosting along my cheeks while his red eyes search mine. "You let him in, little Wynn. Why would you let him in?" My brows pull together, confusion spreading across my face while I try to figure out what he's going on about.

"What you mean to say is she fucked him, brother," Bale sneers from the wall, his fingers toying with a black piece of lace that looks exactly like a pair of my missing panties.

"I'm struggling to see why anything I do affects either of you," I deadpan, my eyes on the material in his hands. He brings it closer to his face, inhaling deeply while the black veins spread from his eyes. The movement should creep me out if they are, in fact, a pair of my missing panties. Yet here I am, so turned on that my upper thighs are becoming slick.

"I love a bit of commando as much as the next girl, but under the skirts? One gust of wind, and everyone is going to see my kitty. Luckily, I shaved." I laugh, watching as Bale struggles to keep his composure, dropping his fisted hand to his side and then into his pocket. His jaw flares as he tenses, his eyes now fixated on the apex of my thighs.

"Don't push him," Luka whispers against my ear, his breath heating my skin. "Stay inside today, this is the only warning you will get."

CHAPTER EIGHT
LUKA

H is heavy footsteps echo throughout the silent woodland, every animal having made themselves scarce with the presence of Satan traipsing through their home.

"Come now, tell me what you boys have actually found out while playing school. I can sense her, the lust pouring from her soul." He grins, his white-fanged teeth on full display. His features mirror mine almost exactly, with his platinum blonde hair and bloodred eyes. He is, in most ways, an older version of me.

"From yours too." He nods at each of us with a smirk. "There have been whispers that another prince has been sending the hounds after the two of you for quite some time, but the murders only started happening weeks ago, correct?"

I nod, confirming what he already knows. "They started happening when we got the news that she had enrolled here. Her parents came to discuss her spot, handed over a donation, and left. The first body showed up the following morning," Bale states, his eyes not leaving the lace in his hands.

He's lucky she's a little weird and seemed to think his new fidget toy was a turn-on.

Our father has always been a little harder on Bale, their relationship strained, even on a positive day. Where I was born with our father's demon qualities, Bale took after our mother. His black hair and amber eyes are identical to hers, and our father despises it. Bale looking so much like her only adds fuel to the already burning fire between the two of them. Her kind are typically more solitary, so as soon as we were born, she left, leaving our father to raise us alone.

We were raised in the Ring of Wrath by our father, one of the Seven Princes of the Underworld. The seven steer clear of each other in the depths unless they are required for meetings or ceremonies. Putting that number of high-level demons in one place, each with their own innate sin, is a bad idea, but letting them all up here together would bring total and utter destruction, which is not something that we can afford.

The chaos of hell is intoxicating for our kind, but in order to keep it from imploding, they live by strict laws. One of which is not bringing disputes to this plane, but here we are. Our father just needs to know more about who it is so that they can sort their shit out where they are supposed to, and the best way to do that is to question the grunts.

"So, they're trying to kill her or take her? Do we know yet?" He questions, his eyes flitting between us.

"None that we have captured have been willing to say much, other than the fact that we're fighting a losing battle and to let them have her," I reply, holding eye contact while Bale stares at the ground with a scowl.

Father continues to walk, heading deeper into the woods, with the two of us walking side by side behind him.

"There are two hunters this time. They're increasing in numbers and if we don't fix this shit soon, I will have to send more demons above ground, which I really do not wish to do. I may not like it here, but they will destroy it like everything else they touch. We need the souls from here for us to stay functioning down there. Do you understand how serious this could be if it gets out of hand?"

"Of course we fucking get it, Father. Give us some credit. We know. We're the ones here living through this shit to make sure the gate is safe," Bale snarls, walking over to a tree far from our father and leaning against it, once again fiddling with her black lace as if it grounds him.

Ignoring him, our father stops mid-step, inhaling deeply with a wide, sinister grin spreading across his already menacing face.

"We think one may be fated to her, could it be possible?" I ask cautiously. It's unheard of and doesn't make a lick of sense, but there's no other reason why he wouldn't have killed her on sight.

Suddenly, Bale is off running back toward the academy, a loud squeal suddenly echoing back to us through the trees.

"Get the fuck off me!" She yells. A loud growl ripping from Bale's throat her only answer.

"For fuck's sake," I huff out, jogging in their direction with Father in tow.

Bale has her up against a tree, her feet dangling below her while she thrashes her body against him in a futile attempt to fight him off. His eyes are pools of molten lava, surrounded by thin, black veins, as he stares at the tears rolling down her reddened cheeks.

"Bale, drop her! You're about to kill the girl!" Father roars, grabbing him by his collar and throwing him to the ground, forcing Wynn to drop into a heap at the base of the tree. "I don't care if you haven't decided or come to terms with the fates, but if what Luka says is true and the hound is fated as well, this is why they're being sent. It's unheard of for a human to be fated with this many different supernatural beings, so there must be something about her that makes her different. Someone wants her to see if they can take it, whatever it is."

I walk over to her slumped form, my hand tracing down her back to siphon some emotion to see where she's at and if she needs some help to calm down. I expected some fear, a little bit of panic with a sprinkling of dread. After all, she is alone in the woods with a demon, a vampire, and Satan himself, but instead, the girl is excited. Her tears were forced from her eyes by Bale's firm grip on her throat, not fear.

She lets out a laugh, her wide eyes taking in the three of us with a hint of humor. "This is a cute little family picnic." She smiles, her brow raising at the laughter erupting from our father.

Standing up, she strolls over to him, a little unsteady on her feet, extending her small, perfectly manicured hand toward him. She's ballsy, I'll give her that. This five-foot-nothing girl just strolled up to fucking Satan to shake his hand.

"Let me guess...You look a hell of a lot like this asshole, so I'm assuming you're daddy dearest? By the looks of it, you already somehow know who I am, but hi, I'm Wynn."

His gravelly laughter fills the air once more, and he takes her hand in a firm handshake, bending down to meet her eyes; the height difference between them is almost comical.

"Hello, little Wynn. You're right. I'm these little assholes' father, but you can call me Satan," he quips, a smirk spreading across his face. She is at eye level with his fangs, but still, excitement is all that I can sense from her. "Now, Wynn, how much of this do you know about, hmm?"

"I know that your lovely twins here have been causing me grief and that I'm being followed by something that isn't them. An asshole named Pyro keeps popping up and warning me to stay inside, and there are creatures with embers for eyes watching my window. Now, Satan, my next question. How do we fix it?" She asks, using air quotes when speaking his name, as if she doesn't believe who she's speaking to.

"We tie the bitch up to lure the two that are here. Torture them, sort this shit out once and for all, and then send her the fuck away from here," Bale snaps, pacing behind us.

"Well then, get to work, boys. I can't be here for this, as you know, but report back in the morning. I hope you live through this, Wynn, but if not, you're welcome down in the depths. You'll fit in well down there. I can see why the fates picked you for these two, or should I say three? You have a fire in you that most humans simply can't possess."

Bale stays at a distance, glaring at her with a scowl. He's fighting this, fighting her better than I'm able to.

"So what's the plan? Testing out a little rope play?" She laughs, her eyes lighting up like we've given her a gift.

"No. We string you up and lure them both out. You can watch us torture them, tear their hearts from their chests, and then we'll send you on your merry way," Bale growls before prowling off through the trees with a sinister grin.

"What he means to say is, yes, Wynn. We're going to play with some rope, and you, pretty girl, will be the bait." I walk over to her, jutting my chin in the direction of the Academy. "Now let's go get you cleaned up and changed."

BALE

The fire mutt is leaning against the hall beside our door, his fire-filled gaze pinned on mine as I approach. I don't have the time for this bullshit, especially without Luka here as a buffer.

"Sorry, Fluffy, no pets allowed. Now get the fuck out."

"As much as I would love to tear your arrogant ass to shreds, Bale, I'm here to help. I know Lucian is here, hunting her. I also know that there are likely more being sent in because I went against command and didn't bring her back for him or kill her." His jaw is clenched, anger clinging to every word he speaks. "I can't explain the pull I have to her, but we don't have the time to fuck around and figure it out. What's the plan?"

We don't have the time to linger on how much of a mess things have become, not now with Wynn being prettied up like a sacrifice as we speak.

Unlocking the door, I walk into the large, dark space we call home. It's more of a wing than a room, thanks to Father and his ties to the place, with a lounge connecting the two bedrooms. Every surface is black, down to the stained timber furniture.

"Come in, but touch anything in here and I will rip your beating heart from your chest. I don't want a flea infestation or some shit."

His laugh is gravelly, echoing throughout the room, with small wisps of smoke leaving his body with each movement. "You ARE aware that we're not wolves or dogs, right? Not even close."

"Looks like a dog. Smells like a dog. Acts like a dog." I nod, emphasizing each phrase. "Sounds like a dog to me."

He leans his back against the door casually, keeping a safe distance despite our current conversation.

"Wynn will be tied in the woods for wolf boy 2.0 to sniff out. Then we question him, have some fun, and send him to purgatory with the others. Now that you're here though, you would have some of the answers we need anyway," I state, walking toward my bedroom to grab two lengths of rope from the duffle under my bed that we usually take hunting. "Why don't you tell me why hellhounds have been tearing students to shreds and hunting Wynn?" I call out, wrapping the lengths of rope around my hand tightly while I walk back into the lounge.

"Look, Bale, I know limited information. Hounds don't get let loose here often, until lately, because Lev knew she was coming, and most are unhinged. They would have been ripping people apart for the fun of it. As for Wynn, I was sent as a test. One I failed. I was to take her back to Lev or kill her on sight because of the fates. That's all I know," he admits, the flames in his eyes burning brighter as he talks about her.

"Alright. I don't like you, not even a little, but it could be of some use to have you there. Don't approach Wynn, but circle at a distance just in case he sends more. Once we deal with the rejected wonder pup, we can regroup and try to figure out what the fuck is going on." I scowl, crossing my arms across my chest with the rope dangling from my hand. My jaw clenches, fangs painfully piercing through my inner lip and spreading the metallic taste of blood through my mouth.

"Just keep her safe. I know you act like you hate her, but keep her safe. I'll be there in the shadows, but do not fuck this up and put her at risk," he growls, stalking out of the room.

"I will protect her with my life," I whisper under my breath and make my way to her room.

CHAPTER NINE
WYNN

My arms are pulled above my head, yanking the hem of the already short dress Luka had picked to skate along my upper thigh. The slight wind is cool against my exposed core, my panties still firmly in Bale's possession.

"Remember the plan. Nothing we say in front of it is true, okay? If he suspects we have any interest in you, even a little, we risk him killing you straight away," he says, expertly tying off the rope.

"Aw, cute. Acting like you care, how sweet. If I didn't chase the high that fear brings, I wouldn't be tied up to this tree, Luka. This shit is exciting." I laugh, the movement causing the tree to scrape painfully along my back. I can feel droplets of blood cascading down my spine, gathering in the fabric that hugs my hips tightly.

Luka pauses, his eyes tracking down my thighs intensely while he ties my ankles to the tree tightly. I find myself staring at him while he's on his knees and gripping my ankles with his searingly hot touch.

I feel a pull toward both of the twins, like my body craves to be closer to theirs the more I'm around them. It could be the danger of them drawing me in, the thrill setting my body alight. Maybe it's the darkness that consumes me when I'm near them. Whatever it is, I'm quickly becoming addicted to the feeling.

Luka's grip on my ankles tightens, pulling me from my train of thought and back to the man staring at my bare core, which would be on full display from his position. A familiar heat begins to build under his intense gaze before two sharp, black points tear through his t-shirt along his shoulder blades.

Holy shit. Why is that so fucking hot?

"Little Wynn, I'm going to need you to do something for me, okay? I need you to think of something mundane. Something you dislike, like unicorns or some shit, knowing you, but definitely something not pleasant. At all." His eyes are locked on mine, with not a hint of humor crossing them.

"Unicorns? Are you on crack, Luka? Your dad is literally Satan. Surely he can afford rehab. Wait, do they have drugs in he—"

Suddenly, he rises from the ground, his lips ghosting across mine. My body attempts to move forward, to close the distance between us, only to be restricted by the rope holding me in place. Just out of reach.

"Because it's taking all I have to not rip this dress off your body and fuck the soul right out of you."

He presses one hand to the tree beside my head while his other hand trails up my side, wrapping around my throat with force before his lips crash against mine. The kiss is consuming, my entire body feeling the heat radiating off of him. Tears prick at the corners of my eyes on contact, the overflow of emotion becoming too much to hold in.

"Fuck, Wynn," he curses, pushing off me and stalking away. My brain short-circuits for a moment, I'm too stunned to speak or call after him even though I want to. I wanted to feel his hands on my skin and around my throat. I wanted to be consumed by him, all from a single taste.

Bale emerges from the treeline, his painfully gorgeous face set in a permanent scowl as usual. "We'll be around, waiting for the moment to intervene. Don't be an idiot, and you should live to see another day."

I've been here for hours, my shoulders aching from the re-straints and a burning pulse shooting through my muscles.

There has been no movement since Bale stormed off in a huff, the bustle of the leaves being the only noise in the otherwise silent woods. My skin feels like ice, the dress doing nothing to combat the cool night air howling through the trees.

Finally, I faintly hear sticks snapping as an extremely large, dark gray, wolf-like beast steps into the clearing with a snarl. He moves closer to me, smoke pouring from his body with each step. This beast looks like the one from my nightmares, only different. Where mine had orange, coal-like eyes, this one has electric blue eyes, shooting glowing embers into the dark mist as he walks.

A loud rumble sounds from his throat as a long, black tongue licks at his already dripping jowls. "Well, well, well. They kill my brothers but leave my feast tied up in a pretty bow. How sweet," he growls, his voice low.

"Didn't anyone ever teach you not to play with your food?" I spit back, keeping my breathing deep and my heart rate as steady as possible, not from fear but from the excitement thrumming through my veins. The beast laughs manically, his mangy fur shifting with the movement. The one in my dreams looked powerful and sleek, with jet-black fur. He was terrifying but beautiful. This one is not like that in any way, shape, or form.

"You're one of the most delectable gifts. Mmm, yes, I'll be having fun with you before I tear you to shreds. I've heard my brother, Pyro. The way he tastes you. My fucked up little gift."

His face comes closer, his long, white teeth snapping the strap around my dress and tearing it clean from my body, leaving me stark naked thanks to my panty thief. The hound's wet nose runs down my bare stomach, stopping at the apex of my thighs and breathing deeply. I try to shift away, but my body is tied up tight, so all it does is force the tree to dig further into my back.

The fear starts to creep in, and not the kind that makes my core flood. Tremors start to roll over my body as my heart rate gains momentum, almost feeling like it will burst through my chest. *They said they would be here, so where the fuck are they now?*

The pure heat rolling off of his body burns my skin as his teeth slice along my stomach, his tongue swiping along my core with brutal force.

A loud sound cracks above us, and then Luka's large, black wings dominate the space in front of me and behind the beast. He's taller and broader than usual, his body looking like it was cut from pale stone. The leather-like wings tuck neatly behind him, with the pointed tips looking like large, sharp horns from the front.

The hound turns to look behind him, completely unphased by Luka's presence. "Where's baby brother, Luka?" He chuckles, licking his tongue along his jowl. "He's missing the show."

I watch as Luka crosses his arms along his broad chest before speaking. "Oh, he's coming. He won't want to miss this bitch being eaten alive. Although, we didn't think you would be eating her twice. It's not like your kind to play with your chow."

The beast's body shifts, shaking excess smoke into the air as he turns back to face me. His long, black tongue trails from my ear down to my nipple, nipping at the sensitive flesh before he sinks his sharp teeth through my skin. My body jolts as the pain from the bite spreads throughout my chest, the movement only making him bite down harder.

A tear escapes the corner of my eye and runs down my cheek, partially from the pain, but also a little embarrassment of knowing Luka can sense what pain does to me despite where it comes from. I can feel the dull throb forming in my core, the familiar ache building in a situation where it really shouldn't be.

Luka's hazy, red eyes rake over my bloodied body, his face impassive while he assesses the damage until his eyes land on the deep cuts through my stomach. I scream out in pain, my body thrashing in the tight bonds and causing them to tear into my skin. It hurts, but it's nothing compared to the ache radiating through my chest.

The hound chuckles, looking up at me with a wide, manic grin plastered across his face. My blood has stained his white teeth pink, marring his face with dark red patches.

"They dragged you out here against your will, tied you up with rope, and left you here to die, knowing that I would find you. Do you really think they will save you now, you pain-hungry little slut?" He laughs, the smoke burning the back of my throat and making me cough when I take a deep breath.

Out of the corner of my eye, I see Bale moving out of the darkness. His body is huge, stacked with muscle in his black, fitted t-shirt and ripped black jeans. The black veins around his eyes now pulse, framing his glowing, amber eyes terrifyingly as he takes in the sight of me.

My heart races, beating so hard that it feels like it'll burst out of my chest any moment as he approaches, stopping right next to the blood-soaked beast.

"I see you found our offering, mongrel. Now, who the fuck is sending you assholes here, and why do they want her?"

The beast turns to face them, with Luka now standing next to his twin and completely at ease. They turn to face each other, a grin spreading across each of their faces in unison. Suddenly, Bale's black, lengthened claws slice across the hellhound's throat, spraying tar-like blood across my bare stomach. It sears my open wounds, forcing more tears to flood my already tearstained cheeks.

"Don't make me ask again, Mutt!" Bale roars in the hellhound's face, holding its jowls in his large hand, before forcing him to face his brother. Luka whips a long, black tail across its face, slicing from its coal eyes down to its snout in one swoop, as though it were tipped with a razor blade.

"You'll die either way. You can choose whether we draw it out nice and long, torturing every single piece of you until you break, or you can tell us what the fuck is happening and we'll kill you quickly," Luka snarls into his face, his voice dripping with venom.

"You little fucking pricks," the hound snaps, causing Bale's clawed hand to tense around his already bleeding face.

"FINE! The Leviathan caught wind that your fated was on its way." He coughs loudly as smoke pours from his wounds. "The demons have been talking. It spreads quickly down there."

Bale's grip tightens, bringing the beast closer to his face. Two rows of lengthened, sharp fangs snap at the beast as an inhuman growl rips from his throat.

"Keep fucking talking." Bale is utterly terrifying in this moment, with his fangs lengthened and his anger targeted. I wonder what they would feel like raking along my skin.

The beast's blue eyes shoot toward me, raking over my bloodied body with a smile tipping his lips. The word fated stands out, instantly halting my thoughts. Fated. Fate is not something I have previously believed in, my parents made sure of that. They are analytical, science-based people with a penchant for the dark and morbid side of the scientific world.

Then again, I'm currently tied to a tree in the middle of the woods with a hellhound at my feet and the twins looking like something out of a horror movie. Yet here I am, wanting to be closer to them, craving the darkness that comes over me whenever they are near.

"Focus, pretty girl, you're going to want to hear what this asshole has to say," Luka calls out, pulling me back to the situation in front of me.

"They say that she will be able to carry young from both of you, creating a hybrid unlike anything Hell has ever seen before. A single being who is a born vampire, demon, an unknown, and human. They will hold more power than any being that currently exists. Do you understand what that means for us? It threatens the entire existence of the fucking hierarchy." The beast coughs once more, the smoke pouring from him turning black.

"We're sent to take or kill her, or one of you, whichever presents itself first, but this little bitch is a lot easier than the two of you. If she lives and you have her, Hell itself will crumble. Lev has a demon versed in the fates imprisoned, and she said the girl needs to die, but you know Lev. He probably wants to fuck her tight little cunt to see if he can breed the bitch too." He laughs, then turns back to the twins.

"Come on now, boys, you may as well—"

Before he can finish the sentence, the beast drops to the forest floor, bursting into flames at my feet. In Bale's hand is a black, still-beating heart, dripping down into a pool of blood on the ground. His chest is heaving as he steps closer to me, dropping the beating heart at my feet.

CHAPTER TEN
WYNN

"Our perfect little Wynn, you did so well for us," Luka praises, walking to stand by his twin in front of me. Their towering forms gaze down, taking in all of the cuts and marks scattered over my naked body. My arms and legs have become stiff, unable to move even slightly within the binds. Luka's hand rests on his brother's shoulder, shifting him to stand directly in front of me.

"Do you really think you can resist her now, brother? Because I sure as fuck can't any longer. I need to feel you, Wynn. I need to taste you. It hurts to not be close to you," Luka forces out, stepping closer to me before running his finger along my wet cheek. He opens his mouth, licking his forked tongue along his finger, and tastes my tears. My body is frozen in place as I stare into the eyes of a demon who looks at me like he wants to devour me whole.

Bale stands beside him, his body tense and unmoving other than his chest rising and falling with each breath he takes. The veins under his eyes are as black as the night sky, pulsing under the surface while his gaze is pinned to mine.

"Tell us. Tell us that you need us just as much. That you feel it like we do. That you love the fucking danger of being around us, Wynn. That every fiber of your being is pulling you toward us," Bale rasps, breaking his silence.

Immediately, I nod, knowing everything he said is true. As soon as I met the two of them, I felt it. The pull, the connection. The need to be closer and know more about them. My body very quickly became addicted to their brand of fear, unflinching when I saw what they truly are.

"There's a chance that this could get a little wild. We're mates, and when mates fuck for the first time, it becomes uncontrollable. With two mates, we're fucking our way into uncharted territory," Luka urges, like that would change my mind.

"Do I need to beg for someone to fucking touch me? I'm the one naked and tied to a tree with cuts all over my body, but you're the ones who seem sc—"

I'm cut off when Luka's hands grip my throat tightly, his face inches from mine.

"Don't say we didn't warn you, pretty girl. Now let me taste what's mine."

He drops to his knees, his tail swiping at the binds on my legs as his large, clawed hands grip my thighs tightly. Raising one to his shoulder, his eyes glance back up at mine, and he winks before settling into place between my legs. Long claws dig into my thighs, keeping me locked in place as rivulets of blood trail down from the impact points. The sharp sting goes straight to my now dripping core, open and exposed in the middle of the woods.

"Relax, little Wynn. Let me thank you. Let me devour you. I had to watch that thing taste what was mine before I was even able to touch you fully," he growls, his long, forked tongue flicking out of his mouth and wetting his lips.

"Look how fucking perfect her cunt is, brother." Bale's body shudders, his eyes fixated on the apex of my thighs as he rakes his sharp teeth across his lower lip, looking like he's ready to pounce at any moment.

Luka moves in closer, the heat radiating from him heating my thighs almost unbearably. His forked tongue traces from my ass to my core, flicking over my sensitive clit with intense pressure. A low rumble vibrates through his mouth as he tastes me, his sharp teeth nipping at my core before he pushes his tongue inside me as deep as he can. Sharp pain shoots through my body as he tears through the last bit of resistance, the orgasm that has been building now threatening to rip me apart.

My whole body tenses while I try and hold it back, not wanting this to end so quickly, and warm tears begin streaming down my face. His glowing, red eyes are now a dark, smokey haze, thick with lust. His claws grip me tighter, the pain pushing me over the edge as a wave of pleasure rolls through my body.

"FUCK!" I scream at the top of my lungs.

My whole body convulses around his tongue, covering him in my release. He moans deeply as he stands, stepping toward Bale, who was yet to move from beside me. Luka raises his brow at his twin, who searches his face before opening his mouth with a grin. Bale grabs Luka's jaw with his tattooed hand, staring at his lips intensely, waiting.

I watch as Luka leans in, spitting my release into his mouth. Bale swallows immediately, closing his eyes and swiping his tongue along his lips hungrily. My jaw drops open, looking between the twins in awe. He just spat my cum and blood into his twin's mouth, something downright filthy to watch, and I have never been more turned on. My core clenches at the thought, craving more.

"Our girl never told us she was a virgin, brother. You couldn't miss out on tasting how fucking sweet she is," Luka groans, wiping his hand across his bloodied chin, and licking the remnants of my release from his fingers.

Bale closes the distance between us, his hand circling the column of my throat as a wicked smile spreads across his face.

"You had the first taste, Luka. It's only fair." He chuckles, moving in and nipping at the skin on my collarbone. His tongue glides across the hellhound bites, smearing the dried blood across my chest and trailing down the cuts on my stomach. He takes a moment, tearing off the tight, black T-shirt he's wearing and tossing it to the side of us.

My mouth goes dry, all rational thoughts that may have been left disappearing in that moment. He's covered in black tattoos, rippling over his defined muscles that tense under my gaze.

"Little Wynn, you do taste fucking divine," he growls, sinking to his knees to lick the slice across my thigh that had been torn back open during the scuffle. "If he wasn't already a smoldering pile of ash, I would tear him to shreds for marking you." He stands then, towering over me once more as he picks me up, forcing me to wrap my legs around his waist. With his free hand, I can hear him pulling his zipper down, his cock teasing at my entrance seconds later.

"Luka, rope." He nods to my wrists, which are raw and bloodied from the ordeal tonight. Luka steps closer, swiping his tail along the bindings, allowing my arms to drop to my sides.

My shoulders are numb and sore from being pinned above me for so long, but in this moment, I couldn't care less. I force them up, wrapping them around Bale's neck as he holds me up by my ass. He eases us both to the ground, with him stretching out beneath me and my knees on either side of his hips being sliced by debris and twigs.

"Bale, I..." I start before he cuts me off.

"Lift your ass, Wynn," he breathes out, pulling me up as he sweeps the head of his cock between my thighs, lining himself up with my entrance before slamming inside of me with one hard thrust. I cry out in pain and pleasure, bracing my hands on his chest and breathing deeply while my body attempts to get used to the feeling of him inside me. "That's it, breathe through it. Focus on me. Focus on how your perfect cunt is taking every inch of me," Bale groans, moving my hips slightly up, then back down, hitting the very end of me.

My core feels like it's on fire, ripping apart at the seams, and I can't get enough of it. The pain drives me forward, my body gaining rhythm and grinding down on Bale's cock with my nails digging into his chest. I can feel Luka's presence behind me right before he wraps my hair around his hand and pulls so that my eyes are looking straight ahead.

There, in the tree line, is the hellhound from my nightmares, staring straight at us. His body looks like it is alight, with small flames flickering from parts of his fur.

"Focus on the fact that you're being fucked by a vampire in the middle of the woods, covered in blood, and being watched by your fire mutt," Luka whispers into my ear as redness spreads across my cheeks. "He'll keep us safe out here. Now let the fuck go. Give in to it, Wynn."

Luka pulls my ass cheeks apart with a firm grip before spitting and swiping his fingers through it, halting at the tight muscle. I grind back against his finger, chasing what he's wanting to give. He slowly eases his finger in and out, spitting again before adding a second.

"This will hurt, little Wynn. Are you sure?" He rasps into my ear, nipping at my earlobe playfully. I nod, staring at Pryo, who is now sitting in front of us, a low rumble sounding from him. His tongue darts out, licking along his lips while he looks down at where Bale is fucking me. I can feel myself tightening around Bale's cock, my body tensing in their hold as an orgasm tears through me.

"You're so fucking perfect," Bale moans, his fingers digging into my hips as he slows, looking over my shoulder and nodding. Luka's fingers slide out, replaced by the head of his cock pushing into my ass. "Push back into him at your pace. Use my cock to ease the pain," Bale demands as he grips my throat, bringing me down into an all-consuming kiss. It's savage, with fangs tearing at my lips and filling my mouth with blood, fueling my need for them. He breaks the kiss only to pull my head to the side, exposing my neck, and nipping at my pulse point with his sharpened fangs.

Luka tenses his grip on my hip while he pushes through the last of my resistance, sliding in and out of my ass at the same pace as Bale fucks me.

"I want to taste you. I want to take you to the brink of fucking death only to bring you back to life again," Bale whispers before digging his fangs into my neck, hard. It feels euphoric, like I'm out of my own body, floating. The pain is excruciating, at war with the pleasure rolling through me at the same time. Bale lets a guttural groan free, stilling inside of me as a rush of warmth floods my core.

"Luka, why, why are you getting bigger?" I cry out, feeling him stretch at the base, locking himself into my ass.

"FUCK!" He yells, pushing himself as deep as he can, his release pulsing through me.

A feeling like fire and ice colliding spreads through my veins, burning and freezing me from the inside out, forcing me to scream in pain. Tears stream down my face as the world starts to tip on its axis, swaying back and forth blurrily, before my mind goes completely black.

CHAPTER ELEVEN
BALE

I planned to make her run, to scare her. I wanted her running from us, overcome by fear, but the more I pushed, the more she pulled me right back in. Now there's no chance of me getting back out, not now that I've had a taste of her.

Mates or mating bonds are not something spoken about often back home, at least not with me. Luka is the one who needs a queen, someone to sit alongside him and rule should that time come. Yet here we are, mated to a girl who is fated to bring chaos and destruction. I still want to hurt her, to make her bleed for me, it's in my nature being a vampire. Only now, I want to be deep inside her perfect cunt as I do it.

Her body is curled against mine as I walk back to the Academy, Luka and the mutt close behind us, walking in silence. Pyro kept to his promise, something that shocked the living daylights out of me. He kept a safe perimeter around her, watching us a little more closely than I had expected. I could hear him and Luka talking body counts, having had another four hellhounds sent tonight to get to her.

"If you two idiots have hurt her, I swear to Lucifer you'll be paying for it for the rest of your miserable existence," Pyro growls, still in his hellhound form so he's ready if we come across another.

"Relax, she just passed out. She lost a lot of blood and mated with both of us. Nothing some rest won't fix," Luka responds casually, laughing at the snarl he receives in response.

"If I could break up your powwow with Wonder Dog for a moment please, Luka!" I call out, unable to open the external door to our wing with her in my arms.

"Everyone needs to take a chill pill. Wynn will be fine." Luka laughs, pushing past me to throw the door open.

I storm straight up to my bedroom, kicking the door open into the wide-open space. The walls are black, lit only by the orange glow from the wall lamps sparsely spread throughout the space. The black, gothic-style bed head reaches the tall ceiling, with our family crest carved into the middle. I lay her down on the black silk sheets, watching as her chest rises and falls evenly despite what she had gone through tonight.

Luka and Pyro walk in soon after, taking in the sight of her sprawled out and dead to the world. She has cuts marring her porcelain skin, red and angry-looking with blood cascading down either side of her stomach and chest. "Let me heal her," Pyro urges, looking pained at what he's seeing.

"What, let you run your tongue all over her? Nice try, asshole. There are other ways to heal her. I'll give her my blood myself if I have to." I snarl, my hand possessively tracing the bite I left on her collarbone. My mark looks perfect on her delicate skin, the rough edges already starting to darken with dried blood.

"Bale, if you do it, then you risk turning her, which neither of you are ready for. Luka, you can help her emotions and pain, but the injuries will still be there. I'll go through you both if I have to, but you two know as well as I do that all three of us are fated to this little firecracker, and I'll do everything I can to fucking save her," he responds, pinning me with his hard, coal eyes. The energy in the room shifts up a gear, and it takes every ounce of control that I have to not snap.

"Bale, let him help her." Luka nods, walking to stand beside me, his hand touching her skin as soon as he reaches the bed. "Our girl is passed out after having the life fucked out of her and snapping a bond into place with both of us at the same time, yet still, all that I can siphon is excitement. She has zero fear. She is meant for us. All of us."

"Make it fucking quick, Pyro. No lingering where you shouldn't be either. We need to talk this shit out before we end up tearing each other to shreds. Luka, you stay here and keep an eye on this asshole. If I stay, I will end up tearing his spine out, tail first," I order, nodding at Luka before storming out.

I start to strum my fingers against my thigh to the beat of her heartbeat as I pace, needing to move and keep busy to avoid running back into the room and shredding Pyro for touching what is mine.

I can hear his footsteps drawing closer to my bed, falling heavily on the old timber floor. He's still in his hellhound form, his power at its strongest when he's in his natural state. "Fuck me, why is that so fucking hot?" Luka suddenly moans from the room, forcing me to stop dead in my tracks.

LUKA

Pyro looks up from his place between Wynn's thighs with a snarl, baring his teeth at my comment. I shrug my shoulders at his little display, biting back a laugh.

"What? I didn't think I would find a fire mutt licking the blood off my mate's skin hot either, but here we are. Get back to work before Bale gets mad and rips you to shreds."

At that exact moment, the door flies open as Bale charges into the space, his eyes pinned on the scene. Pyro's head shakes before he leans over her once more, running his tongue along the bite on her nipple. Her body reacts to his touch, raising up ever so slightly and chasing the warmth. She isn't quite awake, but she's not out cold anymore either.

He slowly moves down to her stomach, following the trail left by the hound's teeth. A small whimper escapes her as he dips between her thighs, breaking the otherwise dead silence in the room, while her body lightly writhes in the sheets from his touch alone.

He hesitates when he gets to her core, the mix of our releases and her blood likely still dripping out of her right before his eyes. My cock strains against my jeans painfully, watching intently as he internally battles whether to heal her pretty little cunt or not.

"Fuck it," he growls, gliding his tongue through her core before pushing it as deep as his form will allow. A moan rips from her throat at the intrusion, her hands gripping the black silk so hard that small tears form from her nails.

My brother moves to stand beside the bed, his body rigid and alert as he traces his fingers along the bite mark he made on her neck, the only mark Pyro left there.

A rumble suddenly sounds from Pyro, his eyes burning brighter than they were before. It looks as if the embers are alight with fire dancing behind the now reddened coals. Wynn's entire body starts to tremor as an almost pained expression crosses her stunning features. Her breathing becomes labored quickly, her chest heaving with each deep breath she takes.

Bale's eyes are pinned to Pyro's teeth, which are now scraping harder along her stomach as he edges his tongue deeper inside of her. Small droplets of blood start forming on the impact points, drawing all of his attention. Her back arches off the mattress more, pressing herself into his teeth a little harder before she falls apart, covering Pyro's face and chest in her release.

He finally eases out of her, gliding his tongue across the fresh cuts along her stomach left behind by his teeth, before moving from the bed and shifting into his more human form.

She must have come to at some stage, and he had kept her lucid to finish healing her before she woke up properly.

Bale walks over to the large chest that sits against the wall, pulling out a black fur blanket and draping it over her, his eyes constantly flicking to his mark on her skin. He's a possessive fuck, so he would be getting off on seeing her like this.

A deep breath escapes her parted lips as she hugs her body into the fur, settling into a comfortable position and drifting into a deeper sleep if her little snores are anything to go by.

"Well, that was hotter than I expected," I groan, shocked at what had just transpired. "Looks like we need to have a little chat."

CHAPTER TWELVE
WYNN

I wake suddenly, surrounded by complete darkness, the familiar smell of lingering smoke becoming somewhat of a comfort. My body is covered by a lush comforter that feels like silk as I run my hands around the space in an attempt to get my bearings.

It's clearly not my room, with no visible windows or any light making its way into the space. I can hear voices coming from another room, yelling from multiple people. It's muffled, but it sounds like the twins are getting extremely heated from the odd word I am able to hear.

"Welcome back to the life of the living, Wynn," an unfamiliar voice purrs from beside the bed.

I scramble to grab the blanket, pulling it up to my chest as I sit up. My body feels tired from the movement, but not sore. My neck, on the other hand, stings with my movement as I look around to try and catch any hint of who it may be.

"Don't worry, they can't hear us. I have made sure we have some time to chat."

"Who are you, and what the fuck are you doing here?"

A click echoes throughout the room, followed by a green flame sparking next to the bed, lighting up a man in a wing-back chair. He looks aristocratic with sharp, angular features and dressed in a black tailored suit. The man raises one of his black, manicured brows, toying with the green flame burning from his flattened palm.

"Well, well, well. Aren't you a pretty little freak?" He smirks, showcasing his bright, white fangs. "Now, let's cut to the chase, shall we, as we have limited time. My name is Leviathan. I'm sure you've heard many things about me, and none of them good."

He stands, closing the distance between himself and the bed with one confident stride. His free hand lowers to the fur blanket, running his fingers across the soft material with a cocky smile.

"These boys growing up with a fucking silver spoon in their mouth. Silk sheets and furs? Really?" He laughs, ripping the blanket from me and tossing it onto the floor. His cold, green eyes linger on my bite mark, the only mark that appears to be left on my skin.

I jump off the bed, attempting to cover myself as quickly as I can, but within seconds, the blanket is burning in my hands with the same bright green flame that was in his. The skin of my palms burns, bringing tears to the corners of my eyes. I love pain, but burns are something else entirely.

"Spit it out, what do you want?" I yell, attempting to back away from the man but he grabs my wrist with his free hand and yanks me back. His touch is searingly hot, similar to Luka's, only this touch leaves welts on my skin, not just warmth. I yelp, trying my best to hold it together through the intense pain.

He drags me toward the middle of the room, where a mist forms, creating what looks like a portal of some kind. It has a green hue, reflecting the flame that's still very much alight.

"Walk, Wynn. Walk through it, or I send them all into this space now. I have ten hounds waiting to hear their command any second. Those idiots are no match when they are heavily outnumbered. Walk through it, and rather than kill your mates now, I'll let them die trying to fucking save you." He grins, tugging me closer to the mist. "If you refuse, however, I will not only ensure their death is long and painful, but you will wish yours was too. There are a lot of demons in Hell that would pay good money to destroy the cunt of the woman who could destroy our world one day."

My heart feels like it's about to burst through my chest, the ability to breathe slowly slipping away with each word he says. I'm usually hard to rattle and able to stand up for myself, but this man gives me the gut feeling that he would make good on his promises. His presence is cold and dark, not the type that sucks you in and gives you a high, like the twins and Pyro, but the type that threatens to pull you under permanently.

I stand in front of the mist, able to see the door on the other wall swing open and the three of them pouring into the room. In a split-second decision, I leap forward, my entire body feeling like it's being pushed and pulled in every direction before being slammed into the ground with brute force.

"Welcome to Hell, Wynn. You're going to love it down here."

The end...for now.

Acknowledgments

Firstly, thank YOU for taking the chance and reading my first book. I know how big those TBR's are, because mine is that big I would need to live 10x over to get through it as it stands. So the fact that you took the risk, and opened up Locked means the absolute world to me. I really hope you enjoyed their story as much as I did!

To my ride or dies. The ones who listened to me cry, who let me vent and supported me each and every step of the way. The ones who picked me up on days when I felt like I wasn't enough. Lauren, Rach, Mel and A.K. Without your support, I likely wouldn't have been able to publish this book. So from the bottom of my heart, thank you.

To my alpha readers. You girls were put through the ringer for this little novella and still stuck around. From dealing with my ass all the time, to hour long conversations about the correct use of the word cum, you were always there. A HUGE thank you to Zoe, Gabby, Amanda, Courtnee, Kim, Ashley and Ori for staying with me until the very end.

About the Author

K.L. Steele is a dark romance author from Victoria, Australia. She loves reading dark, twisted love stories and collecting book boyfriends who are a step beyond morally Gray.

She is a bit of a genre hopper when she reads, swapping between monster, bully, paranormal and dark romance.

Stalk Me
I love it!

Facebook Readers Group

K.L. Steele's Readers Group

Instagram

https://www.instagram.com/authork.l.steele/

Goodreads

https://www.goodreads.com/klsteele

TikTok

https://www.tiktok.com/@k.l.steeleauthor

Printed in Great Britain
by Amazon